Murder in the Hot Air Balloon

The Wootton Windmill Mysteries
Book 4

Izzie Harper

ASIN for the ebook: B0CBYSK1TJ
ISBN for the paperback: 978-1-7392189-3-5

For Lexi, the gentlest, funniest, most gorgeous cockerpoo in the world.

Chapter 1 FRIDAY

It was late autumn in Lower Wootton and temperatures were falling. The trees were shedding leaves and the hedgerows smelled damp. In the woods, the calls of tawny owls echoed as they established and defended their territory.

Ellie Blix and her daughter were walking home from an evening at the Rattling Cat pub, where they'd been watching Zoe's boyfriend perform in his band.

Zoe proudly brandished a set of car keys and kissed the fob, a huge grin on her face. 'Independent at last,' she exclaimed to the stillness and quiet of Pennypot Lane, the narrow road which ran round the village green.

'And no more taxi driving for me,' Ellie replied gleefully, releasing her curly hair from of its ponytail. 'How does it feel to have your own wheels?'

'So grown up.'

Her dad had bought her a white Mini. They'd all driven to the pub to give it its maiden voyage and left the car in the car park.

Under the moonlight, the two women crossed the village green. At its edges, the bracken was a sea of burnished copper. The grass was stiff and semi-translucent in the chilly air, speckled with the crystals of the first frosts. After a few days of heavy rain, the duck pond was bulging. Soon, the water would freeze, and children would be out on their skates having fun on the ice. The nearby bonfire was growing by the day, ready for the village fireworks in a few days' time.

The ducks, who were sleepily huddled by the pond, quacked and scattered, startled by Ellie and Zoe's approach. These were the quietest months. Many creatures were in blissful hibernation. Jackdaws lay in communal roosts, while other animals noisily hunted for mates. Fox cubs, now fully-grown, were leaving the safety of their vixen's earth, and were seeking their own territories and partners, keeping the locals awake with their screams, barks and bone-chilling howls.

The evening had been a family celebration: Zoe passing her driving test; her boyfriend playing his first gig. For Ellie, though, it had been a much-needed night off from washing and ironing, after Blix Blitz's laundry manager had slipped on some ice and broken her collarbone.

They'd left Finn and his bandmates still playing. Sylvia, Ellie's mother-in-law, had stayed on at the pub to 'make sure Finn was OK', which actually meant having a night-cap with the village vicar.

Ellie and Zoe strolled in amiable silence along the lane towards the windmill, occasionally chatting and laughing. In the distance, shots sounded. Was it idiots letting off fireworks or was someone shooting?

They passed houses with pumpkin lanterns outside, nightlights glowing inside, and plastic skeletons in the windows. The tarmac was dry and frost crystals twinkled in the moonlight.

'Is Reverend Jackson Gran's new boyfriend?' asked Zoe.

'I have no idea. She's been very tight-lipped. Hasn't mentioned a word to your dad either.'

'She'd be more likely to tell you than him, though.' Zoe tucked her arm through her mother's and pulled her closer.

For many in the village, this was their favourite time of year. Harvest Festival was over. Halloween and the children's trick-or-treating was to come. Guy Fawkes' Night, the bonfire on the green, the fireworks display. Then

Christmas. It was the season for log fires, snuggly jumpers, hot chocolate, and mulled wine.

Someone on a bike shot past, making Ellie and Zoe jump.

'Hooligan,' Zoe shouted.

'Put your lights on,' Ellie yelled after him. All she could see was dark clothes, dark cap, a dark bike.

A large, long-limbed dog lumbered behind, eyes glinting as a streetlight caught them.

She patted Zoe's arm. 'C'mon. Let's get home. I got about four hours' kip last night. I want to get to sleep before the foxes start up.'

When they arrived at the converted windmill which had been Ellie's family home for generations, she said good-night to Zoe and was soon in bed. Rebus, the cockerpoo, stretched out on the rug next to her bed, having decided years ago that he preferred this to sleeping alone in the office downstairs.

Although she wasn't a fan of winter, Ellie loved making her bedroom cosy in preparation. She smiled now as she glanced round it. The cheerful cerise cyclamen on her bedside table. The cocooning round shape of the old windmill. The solidity of the bare, wooden beams in the white walls around her and above her bed. The wafts of lavender from the scented candle. The cream upholstered chair she'd bought as part of her attempts to reclaim the bedroom after Dave's affair.

Ellie switched off the warm fairy lights around her bed frame and blew out the candle. She closed her book and placed it on the bedside table. Switched off the lamp and was soon curled up under a soft white duvet with her hot water bottle, fast asleep, dreaming about fireworks and bonfires. Fizzing sparklers. Hot, buttery jacket potatoes. Mouth-watering hog roast on a spit.

But it wasn't long before a shrill noise woke her: the barks of the foxes. Tentative at first, then increasingly loud and penetrating, their calls unbuffered by the increasingly naked branches and bushes.

Ellie turned over, regretting not having broken up Sylvia's rhubarb clumps in the rear of the garden before the foxes eyed them up for nesting. She wondered what Rebus made of the their cries. Hopefully tonight they wouldn't go on for too long.

But ten minutes later, they were still at it and Ellie was tossing and turning.

Eventually, she fell asleep, back into swirling dreamland in the warmth and comfort of her bed.

The next she knew, voices wrenched her from her slumber. Screams and shouts. Late-night revellers coming home from a party, probably. Rebus gave a low growl and then barked.

'It's OK, boy,' Ellie told him. Still half-asleep, she swung her legs out of bed and got up, shuffling over to the window. Pulling back the thick curtains, she was dazzled by the bright light of sunrise. Somewhere in the distance a seagull cried, the sound carrying across the cloudless sky.

As Ellie's eyes focused, a hot air balloon came into view, an orangey-red ball in the sky with a basket hanging beneath. A woman's voice rang out across the countryside. Must be a celebration. A small group. Two or three people in the basket, by the looks of it, huddled close.

Ellie didn't know what time it was but with a busy day ahead, first interviewing for a temporary laundry manager, and then helping to build the bonfire for the fireworks display, she still felt the need for more sleep.

She squinted to get a better look. Yes, three of them, arms raised. Having a toast maybe? Hopefully, the wind would carry them out of earshot soon.

She shut the curtains, gave Rebus' ears a stroke and got back into bed. The foxes should be done for the night. She didn't want any more disturbances. Perhaps she'd put ear plugs in.

She slid open the drawer of her bedside cabinet and took the plastic box out. Ear plugs weren't her favourite things.

They helped shut out unwanted noise, sure, but she didn't like wearing them as she found it hard to relax, knowing she might miss an emergency.

But Reeby was on the rug next to her, so they'd be safe, and Zoe was on the floor below.

This time, despite her worries, she fell asleep quickly, dreaming about a hot air balloon. It was different from the one she'd seen, a mixture of pink, purple, turquoise and yellow. A bride and a groom, a celebrant, friends and family, all enjoying the happy occasion.

Then she heard a voice.

Muffled.

Someone placed their hand on her. Someone else jumped on the bed.

Ellie screamed; eyes open now.

Zoe was leaning over her, mouth moving, face intense, words a blur.

'What is it?' Ellie asked, forgetting she had earplugs in. 'What's happened?'

Zoe pointed to her ears.

Of course. Darn earplugs.

Rebus was on the bed, wriggling excitedly and licking Ellie.

She sat up, easing the lumps of foam out of her ears, irritated at being woken so violently. 'Did you have to do that?'

'*Yes*. Two people are having a row in a hot air balloon.' Like Ellie, Zoe was in her pyjamas, her hair in a loose top knot. 'Come and see.'

Ellie tried to garner her thoughts. She'd seen a balloon too but didn't know how long she'd been asleep for.

'If the balloon's still there you'll see,' said Zoe. 'It looked quite heated. Do you think they'll be alright?'

Ellie was awake but her brain was fuzzy. 'Was it an or-angey-red balloon?'

'Yes. Shooting up in the sky. The man was shouting. The woman was screaming, and the man was trying to calm her down.' She swiped her phone. 'I took a pic, look. The sunrise was epic.'

Ellie looked at the image. There were two figures in silhouette form. But hadn't she seen three people earlier? 'Let's see if the balloon is still up.' For the second time, she got out of bed and went over to the window, Zoe in tow.

Ellie scanned the sky. The beautiful sunrise streaked across the view. 'It's gone. Unless it's disappeared behind the trees, it must have landed.'

Zoe stood on tiptoe next to her mum, screwing up her eyes. 'I can't see them either.'

'Let's see that photo again.' Ellie racked her brains, trying to remember what she had seen. 'Are you certain there were only two people in the basket?'

'Yeah, Mum. Deffo. They were facing each other and I saw their silhouettes.' She passed the phone to Ellie. 'Just like in the picture.'

Ellie studied the image more closely. It definitely looked like there were two people, not three. Why would they be having a row? Hadn't it been excited shouts she'd heard?

'Are you *sure* you saw three people?' asked Zoe.

This was the thing. *Was she?* She'd woken up and been half-asleep. What if she'd imagined it or misperceived what was there?

The two of them faced each other.

'Because if there were three people in the basket when I saw them, and two when you did,' said Ellie, 'what happened to the third person?'

Chapter 2
SATURDAY

The next morning, it was around ten o'clock when Ellie got downstairs, having finally got back to sleep after seven-thirty. The first thing she saw was a stack of black bin liners and laundry bags, and four ironing boards dotted around the ground floor of the windmill.

'Good grief,' she said in horror. 'Is all that for Blix Blitz?'

'Afraid so,' Zoe replied. 'Some of it was by the door when we came down. Some's been dropped off while we were having breakfast.'

Ellie smiled as she saw Zoe and Finn, who were sitting at the kitchen table. Finn was in a long-sleeved top and was spreading jam onto toast. His short hair was bed-head scruffy. His cat, Mouse, was in the middle of the table, licking his paws and soaking up a ray of morning sunshine, as much at home in Ellie's house as Finn was. A few months earlier, when a schoolfriend had moved in with Finn, Ellie had wondered whether his relationship with Zoe would cool, but they seemed as keen on each other as ever.

Zoe had Ellie's magnifying mirror out from the bathroom and was cleaning the piercings in the top of her ears with solution from a bottle and a cotton wool pad.

'Did you wash your han–'

'Yeah, Mum,' Zoe replied in a sing-song-y voice. 'After ironing three sets of sheets for you.'

'Aww, thank you.' She gave Zoe a hug and then noticed that Rebus was slobbering over a chew on someone's white sheets. 'Reeby! Off there.' She flapped her arms in a shooing gesture.

He gave her the side-eye and reluctantly got up, leaving his soggy chew behind.

Ellie tucked the sheets back into the bag they'd spewed out of, and hid Rebus' chew. For the first time in several months, Blix Blitz had the perfect balance of staff to contracts, and Ellie was keen to get over this blip as quickly as possible.

'Dad dropped off his iron and board earlier. Finn's set it up in the lounge. And Sally left her iron at the front door.'

'Oh, I didn't hear the bell. Must've been dead to the world after being woken up *three* times,' she said pointedly.

'We've put the laundry in the office,' Zoe continued. 'Gill dropped off three more bin liners full. You're going to need a new washing machine and tumble dryer at this rate.'

'Thanks, lovey. I really hope I can get a temporary laundry manager in place today so I don't have to do that. But if the bags keep piling up like this, soon we won't be able to get in the door.'

'By the way, Dad said you can use his machine, and Sally's taken one of the bags of sheets back to hers to wash there.'

'Brilliant. Thank you. That was kind of Sal.'

Sally was Ellie's best friend.

Ellie shuffled over to the worktop, filled the kettle and switched it on to boil. She'd take stock of the laundry situation after breakfast. She couldn't face it now.

'Incidentally, when Dad came round there was a giant gnome outside the windmill,' Zoe told her mum.

'*A gnome?* Where exactly?'

'To the left of the door. Next to the rose. I took a pic. I didn't notice it when we got back here last night. Did you?'

She picked up her phone, swiped it and held it out for Ellie to look at.

As Zoe had said, sitting at the foot of the climbing rose was a gnome, literally half Ellie's height. A smiling, tubby chap with a white beard, in a ginger jumper and a brown waistcoat. A pointy blue hat sat on ears that stuck out. Hands in his pockets.

'He looks rather jolly. Where's he come from?'

'Someone's nicking gnomes from homes in the village, and from one of the graves at the church.'

Ellie's face fell. 'Oh, no. That's *definitely* not jolly. Why are they doing it?'

'We think it's the "travelling gnome" thing.'

'The *what*?' Ellie was only half listening.

'It's where people steal a gnome, take it to famous landmarks and photograph it. Then they send the owner the photo as a practical joke. You wait. I bet a photograph will appear somewhere of the gnome outside the windmill.'

'Ugh. That's a bit mean.'

'Usually, they return it,' said Finn.

'I agree with Mum,' said Zoe. 'It's a bit heartless. I bet the gnome owners are old, and if the gnomes are stolen from a grave, they'll have been bereaved too.'

'I think I've seen that gnome in the graveyard. Is it to the left as you walk up the path? By the old wall?'

'That's the one,' said Zoe. 'The grave is Mr Blackman's.'

Ellie knew Gladys Blackman. She was in her seventies and Blix Blitz had cleaned for her for years. 'Loves her gnomes, doesn't she?'

'It was her husband who loved them, I gather,' Zoe replied. 'Saw them as protectors. In his will he requested one to be put on his grave.'

'Well – I don't want it outside. It needs to go back to the grave it came from.' Ellie walked to the door, Rebus scampering beside her, opened it and peered round. 'It's not there anymore. I'm beginning to wish we had a security camera now.'

'It's OK,' said Zoe. 'The church has CCTV. There's so little vandalism in the village usually, the previous vicar didn't use it. I've switched it back on for Reverend Jackson and shown him how to operate it. He's on a mission to find out who's doing it.'

'That was kind, lovey. Well done. I heard the Murrays had gone to Australia for a while.'

'Yep,' said Finn. 'He's taken over as temporary vicar at St Mary's for the month they're away. Bob and I were there in the week, trimming that massive yew tree. You know, the one that's leaning on the railings round the graveyard.'

'That explains why we've seen more of him,' said Ellie. 'Given you're in contact with him, you two, could one of you inform him the gnome was here?'

She muttered and changed the subject. 'Were you pleased with how the gig went?' she asked Finn.

'Deffo. We've got a set coming up soon at the Windmill too. The new manager emailed me confirmation yesterday.'

The Blixes lived next to the Windmill Inn.

'Great,' said Ellie. 'We can come and support you.'

Finn chatted away about the band, which was a relatively recent formation with his housemate, Charlie Matthews, who worked at the local butchers, and a couple of their friends.

'They even had some groupies, Mum.' Zoe nudged Finn. 'A local hockey team was on a night out and they took a shine to Charlie.'

'It's his floppy, black hair,' said Finn, chuckling. 'It was the same at school. All the girls had crushes on him.'

'*I* didn't,' Zoe announced.

'Bet you did,' Finn told her.

Zoe was shaking her head. 'Nope. Wasn't into boys at school. It was always technology for me.'

Finn glanced towards the spiral staircase and lowered his voice. 'Speaking of *lurve* ... what's going on with Sylvia and the vicar? They were looking quite close in the pub last night, and there was lots of giggling. He left with his dog collar on one side.'

Ellie smiled at the image.

Sylvia's husband had died a couple of years earlier and she'd moved in with Ellie for a few days last Christmas.

'Haven't a clue,' Ellie replied. 'He seems a nice man, though, so if she enjoys his company, I guess we should give her some privacy.'

'He can knock back the white wine too, so they're well matched,' Finn added mischievously. 'He must've made about four trips to the bar.'

Zoe chuckled and elbowed him. 'Checking up on her, were you? She's in her *sixties*. I'm sure she can take care of herself.'

Her comments brought a smile to Ellie's face. She remembered being that age, and how ancient grandparents seemed. 'Age is irrelevant. It's heart-warming that you were looking out for her,' she told Finn. 'Thank you.'

'Okaaay,' said Zoe. 'Should I take her up a cup of tea?'

'That would be kind, lovey. I'm sure she'd appreciate that.'

'And a couple of Paracetamol,' Finn added cheekily as he started swiping on his phone.

Zoe flicked the kettle back on to boil, made a drink for Sylvia and took it upstairs.

'By the way, the local newspaper is meant to be doing a feature on the band and listing our upcoming gigs,' Finn told Ellie. 'I'm just looking for it on their Facebook page. They came to a rehearsal last week and interviewed us.'

The mention of the newspaper made Ellie shudder. 'You didn't speak to Katie Douglas, did you? That woman will kill your music prospects before you've even started.'

Ellie remembered some of the hatchet jobs that Katie had written about people in the village, including Ellie, Dave and others. And how the editor had police contacts who leaked sensitive investigation information to him.

'No-o,' Finn laughed. 'Fortunately, I remembered and made sure she didn't come out. The paper has a new junior reporter, Roxy Cooper.'

'Helen's daughter?'

Helen ran the local hairdresser's.

'That's right. Charlie's just started dating her. We were really impressed. She did a great job. Asked some interesting questions. She's a live music fan and has just finished a journalism course.' Finn scrolled on his phone. 'Ah, nice. Here it is.' He paused while he looked at the piece. 'Oh, wow. They've given us a full page – that's unheard of for a new band. Look, Zo.'

'Gran's getting up,' Zoe said, coming down the stairs and heading over to Finn to read the headline on his phone. *'Local band, The Barn Owls, are taking the music scene by storm,'* she read aloud. 'Lovely photo of the four of you.' She continued reading. *'School friends, Finn Burdett, Charlie Matthews, Rory Adams and Mike Selham, have reformed the band they set up in sixth form.'*

Ellie thought about Katie Douglas. If she'd written the piece, she would have started with something like, *Finn Burdett, surviving son of local adulteress ...*

Zoe got her own phone out to read the article as she walked about in the kitchen, putting away breakfast things and tidying. *'They all met up recently and realised their shared love of folk music was stronger than ever.'* Then she stopped, put the jam back on the worktop and shot across the room to Ellie. 'Oh blimey. Mum, you're going to want to see this. A post has just gone up on the Wootton Facebook page asking if anyone's seen Owen Field.'

'What's happened to him?' Ellie asked.

Owen was her friend's husband and the chef at the pub next door.

'Posted by Anna.' Zoe began reading aloud. *'He left our house at 5am for a hot air balloon ride with his brother and sister-in-law.'*

'No way.' Ellie leaned over Zoe's phone.

'Yup.' She carried on. '... *to celebrate their wedding anniversary. For anyone who doesn't know him, Owen is forty-eight, five foot nine, slender build. When he left home, he was wearing a navy jacket, black jeans, blue Nike trainers and a red jumper.'* She looked up, paraphrasing now. 'Cancelled the balloon ride from the car. Told his brother he was tired and hungry and was going to McDonald's instead.'

'Crikey.' Concern surged in Ellie.

'His car is at McDonald's, but he hasn't been seen there and there's no reply on his phone.'

'Where on earth has he gone?'

'Anna's reported him missing to the police.'

'That's pretty soon – but fair enough, I suppose, if Anna can't get hold of him and he left home five hours ago,' said Ellie. 'Weird his car's at McDonald's but he didn't go in.'

Finn must have been reading the article on his phone too and chipped in. 'Owen's brother has already started searching with a couple of mates in the area around McDonald's.'

'Oh, heck. How awful.'

'The restaurant is on the main road, but either side of that it's open countryside and goes down to the cliffs at St Margaret's.'

The mention of cliffs sent a shudder through Ellie.

'Shall we give him a hand?' asked Finn. 'I'm meant to be helping to build the bonfire for the fireworks display, but that can wait until Owen is found.'

'Don't forget we've got to check the bonfire for hedgehogs and toads,' Zoe added passionately.

Ellie put her arm around Zoe. 'Don't worry. We'll all help with the wildlife check. Best to do it just before they light the fire, otherwise they might return.' She was absorbing the news. 'I've got mountains of laundry to get through and job applicants to interview, but I agree. We definitely should help.'

Anna was a friend of Ellie's as well as her yoga instructor. She was well known in the village for her friendly classes at the church hall. Initially, they'd got to know each other as Ellie's cleaning company did her and Owen's cleaning. Then Ellie had gone along to yoga and she and Anna had had coffee a few times afterwards, bonding over chat about the long hours their police officer and chef partners worked.

Zoe carried on summarising the key points from Anna's post. 'The plan was for Owen to leave his car at his brother's house and go in John's vehicle to the launch site.' She looked at her mum, her face mirroring Ellie's concern. 'It's got to be them we saw in the balloon this morning, surely?'

'It would be a bit of a coincidence if there were two burnt orange balloons up in the same place at dawn.' She paused. 'I wonder if the police will start searching too. It's all about risk assessment these days. I'll call Anna. See what we can do to help.'

She fetched her phone from the table and dialled Anna's number. 'She's not picking up. She's probably frantic. I'd better get dressed and go round there now.'

Chapter 3

Anna and Owen Field lived at Tollgate Cottage, a large white building with a low wall and black railings around it, on the road into and out of Lower Wootton.

Ellie parked in a side road and walked back. The old entrance on the main road, which would have been where people paid their tolls on their way from Deal to Dover, wasn't used anymore. Instead, a new door and porch were on the side of the house.

Ellie rang the bell and waited to see if anyone was in, admiring the pots of purple pansies which somebody had lovingly planted either side of the stone steps and front door. At complete odds with the pretty flowers, a large gnome sat in front of one of them. Long, blue jacket, belted in the middle, pointy red hat. He seemed to be keeping watch.

A woman opened the door, features crunched with concern. She softened when she saw a smiling face.

'I'm Ellie, a friend of Anna's. My family and I saw her post on Facebook and wanted to know if we can help.'

'Hi. Come in.' She stood back, allowing Ellie room to enter. 'I'm Jaq, Anna's sister. Anna's gone out to put up a few posters.'

Ellie entered the house. 'They're always worth doing, aren't they? Even if it just helps her to feel she's contributing.'

Jaq nodded. 'Exactly.' She closed the door and lead Ellie into a spacious kitchen with a sofa at one end.

'Most people in the village know Owen,' Ellie continued, 'and will quickly learn he's missing, but posters will be useful for motorists and walkers, and people who *don't* know him. Is there any news?'

Jaq gave a sad shake of her head. 'I'm making some soup. I don't really know what to do either and at least it'll be something warm for Anna to have when she gets back.' She looked heavenwards in desperation. 'She's convinced something's happened to Owen. It's not like him to go out of contact for several hours like this.'

'Her Facebook post said he went to join his brother and his wife. Where do they live?'

'Not far. They moved to a village between here and Dover when they started as managers at the Windmill Inn. Eythorne, I think Anna said.'

'Ah, right. But Owen changed his mind about going while he was en route?'

'Apparently.' Jaq threw her arms up in the air, perplexed. She repeated what was on Facebook: Owen had rung his brother saying he was going for some food and then back home to bed.

'How odd. Why get up and go in the first place if he was hungry and tired?'

Jaq shrugged. 'I know nothing, I'm afraid. Just repeating what Anna told me.'

Ellie was trying not to be suspicious, but her private investigator's radar was dinging. Something didn't feel right.

'The brother and his wife didn't think much of it when Owen cancelled because he's pulled out of things before,' Jaq told Ellie. 'So, they weren't surprised.'

'What made them think something was up then?'

'They didn't until they got back from the balloon ride, and John rang Owen to say how lovely it was, and that they'd missed him. But he couldn't get hold of him. John then rang Anna who said he hadn't come home, and she hadn't heard from him either.'

'Owen didn't tell her he'd changed his mind about going?'

'No.'

'What did John do?'

'They were then a bit worried and went to McDonald's. Apart from the car, no sign.'

'Perhaps he didn't text Anna to say he wasn't doing the hot air balloon ride because he thought she'd be asleep,' Ellie suggested, thinking aloud, 'and he'd be back home by the time she got up, so there wasn't any point bothering.'

'Maybe.'

'Has *no-one* seen him at all? None of the neighbours?'

'I don't think so, but I don't know who John's asked.' Jaq went over to the stove and stirred a steaming pan. 'It was still dark when they set off so maybe no-one was up.'

'And he left at 5am,' Ellie said. 'That sounds about right. The sun doesn't rise 'til 7.30ish at this time of year and they had to get the balloon laid out and inflated.'

'Apparently, John wanted to be in the air by 7am so they could see the sun rise. He's got the gear to fly at night.'

'And Anna definitely saw Owen leave?' Ellie was aware she was firing questions at Jaq but she couldn't help it. She was concerned for her friend, and once Ellie's curiosity was aroused, it was second nature to go into sleuthing mode.

'That's what she said. She was in bed. Didn't get up and see him off but he gave her a kiss, said goodbye, and told her he'd be back after the balloon ride to get some kip.' Jaq paused, adding, 'He didn't get back from the pub 'til just before midnight, so he was shattered but didn't want to let John down.'

'Why wasn't Anna going with him?'

'She'd already bailed. She's scared of balloon rides.' Jaq pulled out a chair at the kitchen table and slumped down on it.

'He's clearly gone somewhere because his car's at McDonald's. What have the police said? Are they going to set up a search?'

'At the moment they're not doing a land search,' Jaq replied. 'It's early days. I gather they're going to make enquiries, check places he's associated with and speak to family members.'

Ellie felt a tug of sympathy for Anna and John. Police resources were so stretched. They didn't do searches unless the person was vulnerable.

'They said it depends on what manpower they have available,' Jaq continued, 'and the "risk level", whatever that means.'

Ellie nodded. She knew from Dave how it worked. Everyone was devastated when a loved one went missing, but the police worked on a pragmatic basis. It was why so many families began searches of their own, like John had. 'They do a risk assessment, and the person is either low, medium or high risk.'

Her brain was buzzing with questions. She needed to tell the police what she and Zoe had seen, and tell Anna too. First, though, the question that was circling was, 'How are things between Owen and Anna? Are they happy?'

'Oh, yes. They genuinely get on well. Owen adores Anna and they're the best of friends. Always have been.'

Chapter 4

When Ellie saw Anna, she was taping a poster to a lamp post on the main road near McDonald's. She'd forgotten how petite her friend was, but she looked even tinier now somehow, reaching up to get the piece of paper as high as possible. She was ripping at the Sellotape with her teeth and winding it round the aluminium post.

'Oh, Ells, thanks for coming. I missed your call earlier, sorry. Jaq just rang me and said you were on your way.'

'I couldn't leave you out here on your own.'

When news had surfaced of Dave's affair, Anna had regularly brought casseroles and flowers round to the windmill, and taken Zoe out for coffee.

'Is there any news?' It sounded silly, given Anna was putting up posters, but Ellie couldn't help hoping someone had seen Owen or had information that would help.

Anna shook her head, bobble hat pulled down over curly brown hair. Her huge eyes looked frantic with worry. 'I can't take it in. He gave me a kiss. Said he'd be back in a couple of hours. It's like he's disappeared into thin air.'

Ellie recognised the signs of shock. And – although she knew she had to tell Anna what she and Zoe had seen earlier – she wasn't sure whether it was going to add to her friend's anguish.

'I don't even know if posters will do any good,' Anna muttered, 'but I can't sit at home and do nothing.'

Ellie waited for her friend to finish what she was doing. 'I need to tell you something.' She steered Anna away from the road and onto a chalky farm track.

'What?'

Ellie placed her hands on Anna's shoulders and filled her in. Seeing the balloon with what she thought was three people, then Zoe seeing the balloon with two.

As Ellie was talking, Anna stared at her in disbelief, the possible implications of what she was hearing dawning on her. 'Hang on. You saw three people in the basket and then Zoe saw two?'

'We *think* so.'

'That doesn't make sense, surely? One of you must've got it wrong. Could it have been a trick of the light or something?'

'That's definitely possible. Zoe is certain; I'm not. I was half-asleep and the sun was in my eyes. I've seen what Zoe saw. She took a snap on her phone. Two people facing each other. Whether a third person was behind one of the two silhouettes, out of view, we couldn't rule out and you can't see from the photo either.'

Anna clamped her hand over her forehead. 'It's a bit odd. Who went up in the balloon then? Because John and Gail say they did.'

A thought occurred to Ellie. 'Presumably John was going to pilot the flight?'

'Yes. It's his balloon and he's the one with the flying licence. I was meant to go too but I chickened out.'

'Jaq mentioned that. What did John do when Owen said he wasn't coming?'

'He was gutted Owen didn't want to go. It had been arranged for ages, and he and Gail were looking forward to a lovely wedding anniversary celebration. John tried to get Owen to change his mind, but apparently he was adamant.'

Ellie was trying to piece together the information.

'And although John said it now feels weird,' Anna added, 'they weren't worried at the time because Owen's been a bit flaky recently. So, they took the balloon up. They'd got all the gear loaded. It was their special day, and the flying conditions were good. Never guaranteed in the winter.'

'When did they realise something was wrong?'

Jaq had answered this, but Ellie wanted to check what she'd said was accurate.

'When they couldn't get hold of Owen.'

That would've panicked Ellie too. 'That would've been – what? – a couple of hours later? By the time they'd completed their flight and got the balloon packed away? He wouldn't still be in McDonald's eating his bacon and egg McMuffin.'

'Well, quite.'

'Where did the balloon land?'

'On the edge of the nature reserve at Kingsdown.'

'It's pretty marshy up there. It could've been dangerous. Is John an experienced pilot?'

'Yes, very. Does competitions and stuff. Gail's flown with him regularly and although she's not a qualified pilot, she's very experienced too.'

'Oh well – they landed safely. That's all that matters.'

'Yes.'

They were leaning up against a wooden five-bar gate, surrounded by fields of winter corn and barley which stretched for miles.

'Jaq said a police search isn't looking likely. What have they told you?'

Anna shook her head in disappointment. 'They've provisionally said he's likely to be low risk but they've yet to go to the Windmill pub to complete their assessment. They're trying to see if they can get some additional manpower in from another force.'

Ellie had wondered about this. She knew from Dave they would have looked for signs he was intending to leave; for vulnerability factors and any indications he was at risk of self-harm.

'How has he been? I mean, his spirits?' Ellie was sure if the police were hinting Owen was low risk he wouldn't have been struggling with his mental health.

'He's fine. Working hard at the pub, as ever. He's not keen on the anti-social hours, but he loves cooking and developing the menu. He was making plans and looking forward to the future.'

'What sort of plans?'

'The pub owners want to sell the place. John and Gail started there as temporary managers a couple of months ago, and Owen's been thinking about buying a share when the place is sold. He's been having meetings. About finance and insurance, I think.'

'Good that he was making plans.' Ellie paused. Perhaps the two brothers were thinking about going into partnership. 'Being practical for a moment – what about the hospitals? Have you checked with them that he's not there? In case he's tripped over or slipped. Had an accident.'

After mentioning mental health, she tried to make her question sound a bit lighter. She was thinking about the treacherous chalk cliffs along the coast and hoping Owen hadn't fallen off one of them in the dark.

'Yes. That was my first thought. He loves the clifftops. From McDonald's, he could've walked over to Kingsdown and onto St Margaret's. I rang Queen Elizabeth Hospital in Margate, and Ashford General as soon as I got off the phone with John. They're the only hospitals with Accident and Emergency departments.'

'He'll turn up,' said Ellie, although as she said it, she realised she wasn't confident.

'I can't think where he's gone. When I spoke to John, we couldn't decide where's best to look. Owen didn't reach his brother's, so we decided on where his car is, because we at least know he got this far.'

'That makes sense. Then broaden out from here. Given the police said they'll be going to his work, and have been to his home, that'll alert people.'

'Yes. And thank goodness for John. He's worried sick. I'm so pleased he's searching. What I can't understand is why Owen would vanish like this. It's true he's been having meetings at strange times but he's never done anything like this.'

Ellie wasn't sure what to say. Anna knew him best. 'Well, if John's made a start, that's good news. I suppose it's a question of eliminating all possibilities.' She scoured her mind for what she knew about missing persons cases. 'Dave doesn't get involved unless ...'

She changed tack, realising she was thinking aloud and might worry her friend. 'As you mentioned, I've heard him say they usually look in places the missing person has connections with. That's already happening, and you've rung the hospitals so that's good.'

'I'm going to give them another ring in case their admissions data weren't up-to-date when I first called,' Anna added, facing Ellie, tears brimming in her eyes. 'Oh, Ells, please can Blix Investigators help find him? You guys did so well solving the village murders back in the spring and before Christmas.'

'Er ...'

'You know everyone round here. They all trust you and open up to you.' Hope shone brightly in her eyes. 'I'm not suggesting Owen's been murdered but something's happened. *I know it.* He simply wouldn't disappear like this. He wouldn't leave me.' She paused. 'And if he's lying injured somewhere, I want to get to him before it's too late. If anyone's got a chance of finding him, it's you.'

Ellie's instinct was to say yes. To jump in and help the friend who'd been so kind to her. But she, Sylvia and Zoe hadn't taken on a missing person case so far. Were they up to it? It would be different from a murder investigation as there was no crime scene or murder methods to analyse. On the other hand, they would still be seeking out and interpreting clues, exactly as they'd done on all their other cases. 'I want to help but can't promise anything until I've talked to the others. I'll do that as soon as I can. We work as a team so it's as much up to them as me. If we think we can help, we will.'

'Thank you. I've posted on the village Facebook page again, asking for search volunteers. John doesn't know that many people here. He and Gail only moved from Canterbury recently. We need as many people as possible. But, thinking about what you and Zoe saw earlier this morning, what I can't get my head around is, *did* Owen go up in the balloon, or not? If he did, where is he now and why is John saying he went to McDonald's?'

'And if he didn't do the balloon ride,' Ellie added, 'where on earth is he? He's been gone hours.'

'Exactly.'

Ellie couldn't get out of her mind the difference between what she and Zoe had seen. Had one of them got it wrong? The implications were critical. 'Anna, I don't want to mislead you. Perhaps I was mistaken and there were only two people in the balloon all along? John and his wife.'

What she *didn't* want to say to her friend was: what if Owen had met someone at McDonald's and got into a row? If he was having business meetings, he could have arranged one there. Perhaps it had gone wrong? Another possibility was that he'd left Anna to start a new life.

Chapter 5

Ellie had an hour before she had to interview her laundry manager candidates, so she texted Zoe and Finn and asked them to meet her at McDonald's so she could join the search. Anna decided to go too. It was a twenty-four-hour restaurant with a drive-through, a few minutes out of Wootton and a short walk from where Anna had been putting up posters.

On the way, Ellie asked Anna about the gnome outside Tollgate Cottage.

'I hadn't noticed it,' Anna replied. 'How very strange. I wonder who put it there.'

Ellie passed her the KitKat bar she'd bought her from the garage. She was pretty sure Anna wouldn't have thought to eat before setting out.

'Oh, bless you.' Anna smiled as she took it, tore the wrapper and took a bite. 'Thanks.'

Ellie told her there'd been a gnome outside the windmill much earlier too.

'The same one, or–?'

'Different.' She described the travelling gnome craze.

'That's creepy. And mean. I wonder who's behind it?'

'And how they're choosing who to target? It's upsetting for the people who own the gnomes, especially when they're taken from their loved ones' graves, and unsettling for people whose houses they're put outside. Why you … and me?'

'Perhaps it's a Halloween thing?'

'I was wondering that. I'll ask Zoe to do a bit of research.'

When they arrived, Finn and Zoe were waiting for them with Sylvia. They must have collected the Mini from the Rattling Cat car park. They were all wrapped up in coats, scarves, hats and gloves as the frost still hadn't cleared completely.

Ellie joined them while Anna thanked people for coming.

'Zoe and Finn have filled me in,' said Sylvia. 'A few extra people have come to help here so John has gone to his house to search round there. It leads onto the area where the balloon landed.'

'Makes sense to split up and, apart from here, it's worth looking anywhere he could be.'

'George is leading the search here.' Sylvia paused. 'I say "search". It's just a few locals looking for signs of him.' She pointed him out. 'Tall chap by the jeep. Beard. Dark blue beanie. He's one of John's staff from the pub.'

Ellie tucked her scarf into her Parka and did up the top button.

'We know John already checked with McDonald's whether Owen went there,' Sylvia continued. 'Is it worth double checking, since we're literally on the spot?'

Like Ellie, Sylvia had also been married to a detective, and they both had a strong instinct in situations for things that might have happened and what needed to be done to find out.

Ellie glanced at Anna, who had joined them. She mentioned Sylvia's suggestion.

'No harm, is there?' Anna told them. 'If Owen got there safely, it gives me hope that there might be a good explanation for where he went after that. If he'd been meeting someone, for example, he could've gone off with them.'

Ellie sensed Anna was trying to be optimistic.

'Have you checked at the pub, that he hasn't turned up there?' Sylvia asked.

It was obviously a place he had connections with.

Sylvia was looking round. 'Perhaps he changed his mind about going home to bed, and went straight to work instead.'

Ellie knew Sylvia was keen to be helpful. To give Anna hope.

Anna was shaking her head. 'He'd have told me,' she said. 'He wouldn't leave me worrying. And he'd answer his phone.'

'Fair enough.'

'And Trudy's already rung me. She's the head barmaid. He normally starts at 10.30am and they haven't seen or heard from him. Something's wrong. I sure of it. In all the time I've known him, he's never been late for work. If he'd gone off somewhere, he'd still have got to the pub on time.'

As they were discussing, three more cars pulled up and George went over to greet them. Nick and Charlie Matthews, from the village butcher's, got out of a Land Rover. Sally, Ellie's schoolfriend, arrived with Alan from the village bistro. And Bob Campbell, the local tree surgeon, pulled up in his pickup truck.

An idea occurred to Ellie. She turned to Anna. 'Could you ring John and check what McDonald's told him?'

'Sure.' Anna slid her phone out of her pocket and dialled her brother-in-law. 'Voicemail.' She made sure Ellie had heard.

'No worries. Let's pop into McDonald's and check, then join the search,' Ellie said to Sylvia.

Sylvia nodded.

Anna rang off.

'Have you got a photo of Owen in your phone?' asked Ellie. 'Be useful to show the staff.'

Anna swiped the screen of her mobile and promptly brought up an image. 'I'll WhatsApp it to you now.'

'Brilliant. We'll leave Finn and Zoe with you. I've got staff interviews to do so Sylvia can come back and collect them. Failing that, they can grab a lift with Bob.' She remembered the car. 'What's the make and model of Owen's car?'

'Volvo. It's got a private plate. OWEN5. We passed it on the way in.'

Chapter 6

Ellie and Sylvia quickly found Owen's car in the car park at McDonald's.

Sylvia scanned the immediate area. 'There's no CCTV covering this area.'

'Just what I was thinking. Do you think it's an accident he parked here ... or ...?'

'Hmm. It seems odd when the car runs a greater chance of being nicked or vandalised.'

'Well, whatever was going on, at least we know he came here.'

'I hope so. But I'm finding it hard to get my head around the whole situation, aren't you? Would someone really set off for Eythorne at 5am, decide not to go on a hot air balloon ride with their brother and sister-in-law to celebrate their wedding anniversary and go to McDonald's instead?' Sylvia's eyebrows were arched in disbelief.

'Perhaps he didn't want to go?' Ellie replied. 'Only managed to come out with it at the last minute.'

Sylvia was nodding. 'That's a possibility, isn't it? Especially since it was his brother's wedding anniversary. He probably didn't want to let them down.'

'Except he'd need a pretty big reason, otherwise surely he'd just grit his teeth and go.'

'I'm trying to think what the options are. He could've made an excuse and saved himself from getting up at 5am or told the truth and said he didn't want to go. Anna said he got back from his pub shift at midnight, so it would make sense he was tired. That's five hours' kip. I wouldn't be going anywhere on that.'

Ellie rolled her eyes affectionately. Sylvia had the ability to sleep anywhere, regardless of light, noise or comfort. 'Or – perhaps he *did* want to go – and something more important cropped up?'

'One of the problems is we don't know for sure what Owen told his brother. We don't have his account. We only have John's, via Anna.'

'Gotta say, five hours' sleep sounds a luxury at the moment,' said Ellie, her voice creaking with weariness. 'I'm sure the foxes are digging in that flippin' rhubarb of yours. It's quadrupled in size since you planted it. Nice, quiet spot by the wall. Perfect place for an earth underneath.'

'Let's sort that out then. Break it up.'

'Last night it was the foxes first, then shouts from the hot air balloon and then Zoe waking me up. Reckon I got about four hours max.'

'You can join me in a granny nap later,' said Sylvia, giving Ellie a nudge.

She rolled her eyes and joked, 'Is this what my life has come to?'

'Actually, they were talking about rhubarb on Radio 4 the other day. November's a good time to dig it up. If the foxes haven't already dug an earth, let's do it this afternoon. Break the clumps up and leave it out for a bit. That's what the lady on *Gardener's Question Time* said to do.'

'Oh, joy. Something else to do when I get home,' said Ellie rather grumpily. 'Think I'll see if I can enlist Finn's help.' She changed tack. 'Anyway, we're here now so let's go in. With any luck some of the staff from earlier might still be on shift.'

They made their way to the restaurant entrance. A few moments later, they were talking to the manager, Ryan, a twenty-something man with pimples and sweaty skin, in a grey uniform.

Ellie showed him the photo of Owen Field on her phone. 'We're looking for our friend and believe he might have been here earlier this morning just after five. Were you here then?'

He nodded.

'Do you recognise him? He's missing.'

The manager shook his head. 'We were very quiet then but one of my staff had to go home as her boyfriend had locked himself out, so I was on one of the tills. I'm pretty confident your friend wasn't here.'

'How long were you on the tills for?'

'A couple of hours. I had to wait until a new staff member arrived and then I went back into my office. So, if he was here between 5am and 7am, I should have seen him, but I really don't think he was. You're welcome to ask the staff.' He pointed at a long, stainless-steel worktop where a conveyor belt of young adults was packing food and placing it in racks. 'They were all in earlier and would've seen him if he'd come in.'

'OK. Thanks. Finally, the parking places by the hawthorn bushes...?'

He frowned.

'On the way in. Near the flowerbed.'

'Oh, yes. What about them?'

'Our friend's car is there. We couldn't see any CCTV in that area. Is that right?'

'Unfortunately. It's company policy only to cover the busiest parts of the car park. Otherwise, it's too much to monitor every day.'

'If I email you this photo, could you ask the rest of the staff if they saw him?'

'Sure.' He gave Ellie his email address.

She sent the picture over to him, thanked him for his help and she and Sylvia made their way back to the car.

'Curiouser and curiouser,' said Sylvia 'Where did Owen go then? And why tell his brother he was coming here?'

'We need to speak to the brother, don't we?' Ellie checked her watch. 'I've got to go and interview these laundry managers. Would you be alright to talk to John yourself?'

'I can do that. No problem. What do we know about him?'

'Not much at all. He hasn't lived round here until recently.' Ellie told Sylvia about the pub in Canterbury and about John being made manager of the Windmill Inn. 'Anna's husband, Owen, has been the chef at the Windmill for several years. Popular, really good at his job and a nice bloke...'

'... and all of a sudden, his brother's in town and running the pub. I wonder how Owen felt about that, or was he happy being a chef?'

'They got on well, I think.' Like Sylvia, Ellie had been wondering if there were tensions or they'd had a row. A fight, even. 'I have to admit, some of those questions have been going through my head too. Anna said Owen wanted to buy a share in the pub.'

'That's good. Hopefully, this is a temporary blip.'

'Yes – at the moment he's just missing and may very well be fine. So, I know we've both got over-active imaginations, but let's try not to get ahead of ourselves.'

'Fair point.'

'Perhaps the most useful thing would be to speak to John, see what he has to say, and continue helping with the search. If Owen doesn't turn up, we can start asking different questions.'

'I agree. You can tell we've both been married to cops, can't you? We're immediately assuming the worst.'

Ellie gave her an understanding smile. 'Can you text me? Let me know what John says?'

Chapter 7

When Ellie pulled into the drive at the windmill, she saw a new board outside the pub next door, listing all the game dishes they were serving now. A rickety black bicycle leant up against it. The front door of the pub was open and lunch smells and chatter wafted out along with the gentle beat of music.

As soon as the windmill's front door came into view, Ellie saw a fresh mountain of laundry bags and bin liners. Some from her cleaning staff, some from clients.

She was going to have to ask them to leave them in the outhouse, where the washing machine was, otherwise they soon wouldn't be able to get in the front door.

Five people were waiting for her. A young woman Zoe's age with a nose stud, who Ellie had seen in the pet shop. A woman Ellie recognised from the choir. Sang alto. Another woman who'd lived in Lower Wootton as long as Ellie remembered. Nora? Cora? Something like that. And two men who looked as though they were related. The older one Ellie recognised as 'Sarge', who the Blixes had got to know on a previous investigation. He lived with a nephew. Perhaps this was him.

'Morning, Mrs Blix,' Sarge drawled in his country accent. 'Young lad came along. Saw all your bags of washing and turned on his heel.' He chuckled and nudged the chap with him.

Ellie smiled at the five of them. 'You can't be here about the laundry job, Sarge, surely?'

'I most certainly am. Sean and I are going to do it as a job share. Lives with me, he does.'

Cora-Nora tutted loudly.

'We need a new boiler.'

Ellie shuddered as she remembered last winter when their boiler had kept going on the blink. Someone of Sarge's age, it was no joke being without heat.

'Going to have to find the money from somewhere,' Sarge continued. 'Something I can combine with my shifts at the garden centre and Sean can fit round his new business.' He eyed up the wayward branches of Ellie's wisteria in the garden. 'That needs a good pruning, Mrs Blix, it does. Twice a year. Take all those whippy growths back to five buds.'

Ellie had no idea what whippy growths were, and it was winter. There weren't any buds. But she smiled anyway, and muttered, 'Hmm, yes.' She stacked the bags to the side of the door and opened up.

Sarge carried on surveying Ellie's garden. 'You haven't been struck by the gnome stealer then,' he said in a low voice.

'How strange you mention that. Someone put one outside the windmill earlier.'

'That'll be on Facebook by lunchtime, I bet,' said Sean, nodding at his uncle.

'Ugh. I hope not. You're the second person to say that. What a very odd business it is. Anyway – come on in. The dog is a bit over-friendly, I'm afraid.'

'You tuck yourself in behind me,' Sean told his uncle, 'so he doesn't knock you over.'

'Good Lord,' Sarge exclaimed, his head on a swivel as he entered the windmill. 'It's like a Chinese laundry in here. We'd better get cracking.'

Someone had brought in six zipped laundry bags; large blue-and-white, waxed bags with handles. And ten more bin liners. Two of these had come open and towels and bedding had spewed onto the floor.

One of the towels had been ripped to shreds. Having greeted the arrivals, Rebus proudly resumed his position on it and continued chewing the cotton.

'No, no. Rebus, off there.' He begrudgingly moved and she picked up the torn item. 'I'll be deducting the cost of the towel from your pocket money,' she joked.

Ellie turned and was about to thank her applicants for coming when she noticed that Cora-Nora had wandered off and was looking round the lounge. Ellie followed her. 'Er ... hi, hello?' She got a strange feeling suddenly, her radar going off. 'We're in here ...'

'Oh, sorry.' The woman flickered the briefest of smiles, nothing that reached her eyes. 'Nice place you've got here.'

'Thank you. I don't think we've been introduced.'

'Cora. Cora Reynolds.'

Definite danger vibes.

'You live in the village, don't you?' Ellie was keen to get a handle on the woman.

'The thatched cottage on the road out of the village, by the bridge. The Old Hare and Hounds.'

'I know it.' Ellie certainly did. 'The old pub.' It was a pretty place, semi-dilapidated, and rumoured by some to be haunted. 'We're in the other room.' She gestured to the kitchen, just about managing to resist shooing her.

Once they were all together, Ellie explained about the laundry manager breaking her collarbone. 'I've had to arrange this at short notice so it will be a bit informal. As you can see, we're in a bit of a muddle.' She smiled apologetically. 'Would you like to all sit in the lounge? I'll grab your CVs from the office and–'

'I haven't got one,' said Sarge. 'Sean sent you his.'

'That's fine.' Ellie knew Sarge had worked at the garden centre ever since his accident in the Seventies and, although he did restricted hours, he'd hardly missed a day. 'I'll have a chat with each of you in the kitchen.'

Twenty minutes later, Ellie had interviewed the women. When she went to fetch Sarge and Sean from the lounge, however, they weren't there. Perhaps they'd realised the job wasn't for them after all and had left? But then, from the garden, she heard a repetitive slicing sound, a spade going into the ground, out and back in. She looked out of the window. Sean was digging up Sylvia's rhubarb while Sarge issued instructions.

Ellie ran out, Rebus behind her.

'This lot needs breaking up,' said Sarge. 'Takes over otherwise.'

'Tell me about it.' She mentioned being anxious about the foxes nesting under it.

'None here at the moment but there will be soon enough.' Sarge was leaning on a spade of his own. He straightened up and rubbed his back. He'd suffered a severe injury in the circus. 'Don't fret. Sean'll have those clumps broken up in no time. He's got a good back on him. Not like me.'

Ellie felt a surge of relief. It was a bit cheeky of them to start digging without asking if it was OK. She was obviously going to have to keep an eye on the two of them or they'd reorganise her whole garden. But this would save her from asking Finn to do it.

'He's just finished an apprenticeship, Sean has, and started his own gardening business.'

Over the decades, Sarge had trained generations of staff at the village garden centre. He clearly enjoyed teaching and was good with younger people.

'Can't say I was expecting to see you in my candidate list,' Ellie said to him.

'Sean saw your post on Facebook. Thought, why not?'

'Is Sean the nephew you told us about? Who lives with you?' Ellie wanted to check.

'That's the one. He's my great-nephew actually, but we don't need to split hairs, do we?'

Ellie couldn't help laughing. There was something about Sarge that was disarmingly honest. 'I'm going to order a new washing machine and tumble dryer. And Bob's lent me an old washer from his garage for the outhouse.' She gestured to the single-storey brick building.

'Is there power in there?'

'Yep.'

She explained what she was looking for. She would be happy to help Sarge out and wasn't worried about Sean. But she did want to know the work wasn't going to be too much for Sarge, though. 'What I need is someone to collect and deliver the bags.'

'Righto.'

'To load and unload the machines.'

'Yes.'

'Iron the sheets and shirts. We do a lot of men's shirts. Then fold everything and bag it up for delivery.' As she explained, she wondered which parts Sarge was thinking he'd manage. 'The laundry manager thinks she'll be off for six weeks while her collarbone knits together. So, it's only temporary, mind.'

'As long as I can sit down, I can do the ironing. You've got boards and irons. Sean is going to do the collections and deliveries.' He looked at her and smiled kindly. 'It's my day off at the garden centre. I'm no good doing nothing. If you like, I can get started on this backlog for you?'

Chapter 8

After the McDonald's trip, Sylvia returned to the fields where Anna and the others were searching for Owen. The grass was thawing, and a watery winter sun was stretching out in a blue sky.

'I'm going to go and have a quick word with your brother-in-law,' Sylvia told Anna. 'There are a couple of things I'd like to ask him. What's their house called?'

'"The Vines". It's down an unmade lane, just after the garage on the main road. Manor house type of place on the left-hand side.'

'Righto.'

'It's a good place to search as it leads to where the balloon landed and is where they were meant to meet.'

'I agree. Will you be OK here or would you like us to drop you home?'

Anna shook her head. 'I'd prefer to keep myself busy,' she said sadly. 'At least out here, I feel I'm helping.'

Sylvia collected Zoe and fifteen minutes later the two of them parked at The Vines and got out. They were surrounded by crop fields, extending as far as the eye could see. It was a large, red brick house, double-fronted with a neat gravel path leading up to a white portico door.

Zoe whistled. 'He's got to be loaded to afford this place,' said Zoe. 'How does that–' She broke off. 'Gran, *look*. It's the gnome that was outside the windmill.'

Sylvia hadn't seen the gnome and had been in bed when they were discussing it, but Ellie had mentioned it. 'Are you sure it's the same one?'

Zoe got her phone out and showed Sylvia the photo they'd taken.

'Yes, that's definitely him. I recognise that blue hat and brown waistcoat. How odd. Get a pic of it there, lovey, can you?'

Zoe did as she was told. 'They've got a video doorbell.' She pointed at the silver box in the middle of the door. 'If it's working, it might show us who the culprit is.'

'We can ask them. Need to make Owen the priority for now though.'

'Absolutely. What I was saying was – how does he afford a place like this on a pub manager's salary?'

Sylvia was thinking along similar lines but tried to give John the benefit of the doubt. 'It's hard to tell. We don't know what property he's bought and sold in the past. Or what investments he might have made.'

'Gran, you sound like a financial adviser.'

'Thank you very much. What did you ask the question for if you didn't want to know the answer?'

'Alright. Keep your hair on.' She grinned cheekily.

'Let's see what he's got to say, shall we?' said Sylvia. 'I can see them in the bottom field behind the house.'

'Are you going to tell him we're private investigators?' asked Zoe.

'No. Not at this stage. I know it's difficult to switch that part of our brains off, but we aren't working as private investigators yet. At the moment, we're just here to help find Owen.'

John Field was beating undergrowth with a stick. He was under six foot, wearing a long, olive-green cattle coat. Mousey-coloured hair pushed out of a tweed cap. Quite the country gent.

'We've come to help,' Sylvia told him, giving him what she hoped was a winning smile. 'This is my granddaughter. What would you like us to do?'

A lurcher came bounding over to Sylvia and Zoe, tail wagging.

A man called the dog to heel and put it on a rope lead. He was wearing dark clothes and a grey cap.

'Thanks for coming. Every extra pair of eyes will help. If Owen decided to go for a walk, it's likely he'd have come this way. He loved the chalk fields down to the sea.' John gave a sad smile. 'One of the guys has got to go to work, so if you could slot in on the line and take his place,' he said as he continued to bash the vegetation, 'we can cover the area methodically.'

Was it safe to assume John hadn't heard from his brother since the contact at 5am? Sylvia wasn't sure. Even if he had, Owen was clearly still missing, or they wouldn't be searching.

'Did he call you or text you to let you know he wasn't coming?' she asked, trying to sound as innocent as possible. It was one of the things she was most curious about.

Because text messages left a trace.

'He rang me from the car,' John replied absent-mindedly and pointed to several metres away. 'That's the guy that needs to leave. With the dog. Todd. He's one of my barmen. Do you want to go down there? Take his place. That way we won't miss anything.'

'Of course.'

John gave Zoe a cursory nod.

Zoe whispered to her gran, 'I'm sure that's the guy who shot past Mum and me on his bike last night when we were walking home from the pub.'

'I've seen him in the woods with his dog,' Sylvia replied. 'His mother lives in the thatched cottage at the end of the village. By the stream. She does bell-ringing at the church with me.'

Sylvia also wanted to know how things were between the two brothers, but now wasn't the time to ask questions. And fair enough. The man's brother had gone missing and finding him was the priority. They'd be able to find out from Anna what the relationship was like.

Sylvia and Zoe took up their position in the search line and the barman left with his dog. They had reached the edge of the golf course now and the terrain had changed from crop fields and hedgerows to a marsh landscape with ponds and dense patches of rush, sedge and reeds. In a fenced area, a herd of cattle grazed, oblivious of the search that was underway.

John cleared his throat. 'This stretch is going to be much more challenging,' he shouted at everyone. 'You need to be careful not to slip or fall. We don't want any accidents. Let's all keep an eye on the people either side of us so that everyone stays safe. Yes?'

There were replies of agreement.

Much of the ground was waterlogged. In the distance a wooden bridge straddled a wide waterway. Along its edges were thick banks of mud. There were plenty like these along the creek in Faversham and Saltmarsh. One foot on them and you sank straight in. Zoe knew too. She and Finn had had a near escape trying to rescue Rebus one Sunday when he took off after a duck and landed on his belly, sinking quickly before Finn grabbed him.

'What if Owen went walking and fell into the water?' Zoe whispered to Sylvia. 'Or that mud?' She snapped a few shots on her phone.

'I know,' Sylvia replied. They'd heard that Owen liked this section of the countryside. 'I'm trying not to think about it. I'm quite sure it's occurred to John, too.'

'I'm glad we came prepared, aren't you?' Zoe asked Sylvia as she pointed at her walking boots and thick socks.

Sylvia briefly put her arm round Zoe.

'I'm going to look up the *What3Words* reference for this place.'

'What three what?'

'It's a way of identifying a precise location–'

'Like an ordnance survey grid reference?'

'Yeah, Gran.' She rolled her eyes. 'But a twenty-first century version.'

On the ground at the edge of a ditch, a cluster of speckled redshanks clicked and tweeted. Sylvia recognised their distinctive red legs and long bills, probing the mud. The sun had disappeared behind clouds and, overhead, skeins cut across the grey winter sky.

Behind them, a marked police vehicle pulled up. Officers got out and began striding towards them.

Sylvia knew it meant something had happened, or the police needed information. Could it be good news? Alternatively, if they'd found a body, officers would have gone to notify Anna. Perhaps these guys had come here to inform John.

Chapter 9

While Sylvia studied the police, Zoe took out her phone and dialled her mum.

'How's it going?' Ellie asked.

'The cops have just turned up. They're talking to John Field.'

'Any indication of whether it's good or bad news?'

'No. Should we come home? Finn and I said we'd do a few more loads of laundry for you.'

'That's kind. Thanks, lovey. I'm hoping I should be OK. I've got Sarge and his nephew here at the moment. They've plumbed in Bob's old washing machine, and have set up an operation in the outhouse.' She told Zoe about the interviews.

'Oh my goodness. That's hilarious. Wait till I tell Gran.'

'But I've just had a call from Anna. She's desperate for us to start investigating. She's on her way over so it would be useful for you and Sylvia to be here too.'

'Cool.'

'Before you leave, though, can you tell the police what we saw this morning?' Ellie realised that, with all the flap about the Blix Blitz laundry and talking to Anna, she hadn't got round to telling them. 'Unless other witnesses saw the balloon, they won't have that information to use in their decision-making.'

'Yeah, Mum. I'll tell them everything. But they'll probably want to talk to you as well.'

—ee—

After Sylvia and Zoe had spoken to the police, the two women drove back to the windmill. Bob Campbell, Finn's boss, was just leaving, having given Finn a lift home.

Rebus charged over to greet them, wriggling and squealing as though he hadn't seen either of them for centuries.

Zoe slid to her knees and enveloped the dog in a big hug. 'Hey, boy. Did you miss us?'

The house looked completely different now that all the laundry bags, irons and ironing boards were in the outhouse. Ellie and Finn were sitting round the kitchen table.

Ellie's face was serious.

'Still no sign of Owen?' Sylvia asked.

'No. And poor Anna is distraught. She could barely get her words out on the phone.'

———ell———

Twenty minutes later, Anna arrived. 'Sorry I'm a bit late,' she said when Ellie let her in. Her voice was trembling and flat, and her face was white. 'I popped into the pub next door on the off chance someone had heard from Owen.' She screwed up her face in disappointment. 'Nothing,' she said with a sob.

'Oh, sweetheart. Come in. Let's get you a cup of tea.' She steered Anna over to the table.

Rebus positioned himself next to Anna's legs, resting his paws on her knees so he could lick her.

Zoe went to fill the kettle.

'Whose is the bicycle outside the pub, leaning on the board?' Ellie asked as she hung up Anna's coat.

'The black one?' asked Anna. 'George's, I think.'

'Perhaps it was him who shot past Zoe and me on a bike on Friday night?'

'He does a lot of exercise. He's a marathon runner so he's always training for something.'

They were soon discussing Owen's disappearance.

'Earlier I mentioned I'd value Blix Investigators' help,' Anna said as she took a sip of tea. 'Have you guys had a chance to discuss whether you can? The longer Owen's missing, the more convinced I am that something's happened to him.'

Sylvia replied first. 'We haven't yet, but can you explain which aspect most makes you think something's happened to him?' She paused and softened her voice. 'Is there anything you're not telling us?'

'No, no, not at all. It's just that, unless he's hurt somewhere, he wouldn't disappear like this and make us all worry … or not turn up at work. It's not in his character.'

Ellie was listening to Anna's response to the question. The logic made sense.

'Before we agree to help,' said Ellie, 'can I check that the police have now completed their risk assessment?'

'Yes.'

'And they've definitely categorised him as a low risk missing person?'

'Yes.'

'And they haven't started searching?'

'No.'

'That should make it fine for us to investigate his disappearance then. What do you think, team?' She looked at Sylvia and Zoe.

'Fine by me,' said Sylvia.

'What she said,' Zoe said, pointing at her gran.

'Good,' said Ellie. 'That means we need to have a team meeting as soon as possible. We haven't carried out a missing persons investigation before and it would be useful to agree on our strategies and priorities.'

Anna cupped her hands over her nose and mouth, tears streaming down her face. 'Thank you. I feel so much more confident already, knowing you guys are going to help.'

As Anna was talking, Ellie felt a growing desire to know more about how Owen lived. 'Could we come and have a look round at your house? Obviously, the purpose would be a bit different from the police's visit. I would like to get an idea of what your husband's life was like, and your life together.' Ellie knew Anna's house reasonably well from cleaning it, but that was mainly the layout, the flooring, where the bins were. What she wanted was to have a bit of a nose, a more close-up study of Owen and Anna Field.

'Sure. Whenever you like.'

'How about now? No time like the present. The sooner we can understand where Owen went and why, the sooner we might be able to find him.'

'That's true, you know,' said Sylvia. 'John and his gang are doing a good job of scouring the countryside but at the moment no one is piecing Owen's last movements together, and what was on his mind.'

At that moment, there was a loud click. All the lights went off and the windmill was plunged into darkness and quiet. No humming from the fridge. No whirring of the fan on the oven. The fuse board had tripped.

Chapter 10

Half an hour later, the three Blix women were at Anna's house on their background-finding mission. As Ellie suspected, the gnome had gone from the front of the building.

They'd left Finn at the windmill connecting one of Bob's extension leads from the main building to the outhouse, where all the high voltage machines and irons had overloaded the ancient wiring in the windmill.

Ellie was in Anna's lounge, her mobile stuck to her ear, hoping that electrician number four would answer his phone and be able to help them out.

Anna and Jaq had nipped out with two old sheets to tie on the railings of the bridge over the road by McDonald's. On them they'd written, 'HELP! HAVE YOU SEEN OWEN FIELD?' Ellie was pleased they weren't at home, as it meant that she, Sylvia and Zoe could look around freely.

Sylvia was in Owen and Anna's bedroom, and Zoe was in the kitchen.

The lounge was exactly as Ellie remembered it. A large room with white walls, cream curtains and carpet, two four-seater sofas in cream with two matching armchairs. French windows opened onto a patio and the garden. A wood-burning stove glimmered orange in the fireplace.

Ellie had been here as a guest a couple of times. She and Dave had had drinks and dinner with Owen and Anna and, after Ellie and Dave split up, the two women had had girly nights together on several occasions. Takeaway, film, wine. By far the majority of times Ellie had been here, though, was as a cleaner. Then, her focus had been different. It had been thinking about which furniture needed moving; when the freezer had last been defrosted; whether the mirrors needed cleaning; if there were enough logs for the fire.

Now, though, she needed to take her cleaner's hat off and put her private investigator's one on.

Plenty of photos on the mantlepiece above the fire. More photos on the walls. Anna and Owen sailing together, on holiday, walking in the woods. Cake and candles, someone's birthday. Smiling, relaxed, happy. So, what had happened? Had there been an accident? Had he left Anna? Had he been abducted or murdered?

Ellie made a visual sweep of the room, relieved that her friend wasn't here to witness her life being examined. On a coffee table by one of the squishy sofas, there was a paperback novel, a bottle of funky green nail varnish – Anna's favourite – a tube of hand cream and a hair scrunchy. By the other sofa, there was the latest edition of *Chef & Restaurant* magazine, a set of nail clippers and a stress ball. How lovely to have so much space to spread out.

In the corner of the room, underneath a wooden sideboard, a wicker paper basket was stuffed full of paper. Posters, probably, which hadn't printed properly. One of the sheets of paper caught her eye. The lettering wasn't large, as a poster might be. It was lines of dense text, in a small font. Ellie gave it a tug and, before she knew it, the entire contents of the paper basket had come out on the carpet. Pages and pages of what looked like a contract.

She picked up one of the sheets and skim-read the text.

'The Rattling Cat, Lower Wootton.
Sold by: Hawkshill Brewery Ltd
To: Owen Andrew Field
Purchase price: ...'

So, Owen was buying the pub at the other end of the village. And would be in direct competition with his brother at the Windmill Inn.

What had happened then?

Ellie suddenly felt uncomfortable. Having a look round to get a general sense of things was different from reading her friends' private documents, so she bundled the paper back into the basket and picked up her phone to try the next electrician on her list. She was leaving a message on yet another answerphone as she walked into the kitchen to join Zoe and Sylvia.

'Still no luck?' asked Zoe.

Ellie shook her head. 'That's six I've tried. Why don't these tradesmen answer their phones?' She took in Anna's kitchen. It was spotless. Gleaming quartz worktops and white tiles.

'Do you want me to try Brian Douglas?' asked Zoe. 'I know you hate Katie but he's a really good electrician.'

Brian was Katie Douglas' son, Ellie's *bête noire* from the local paper.

'Might have to eat humble pie and give him a go.' She pulled a joke crying face.

Zoe held up a damp, ink-smeared Post-it, with a handwritten poem, signed, 'O.' 'This is cute. Owen left Anna lil' love notes, look.'

'Where did you find that?'

'It was on the floor by the washing machine.'

Perhaps it had dropped out of a pocket.

Sylvia looked relieved. 'Ah. See? Romance isn't dead.'

'There's a pair of fingerless gloves on the microwave,' Zoe added.

'Perhaps Owen meant to take them when he left for the balloon ride,' said Sylvia. 'It was silly o'clock.'

Ellie told them about the purchase contract in the bin. 'Did you find anything upstairs?' she asked Sylvia.

'Come up and have a look,' Sylvia replied.

The upstairs landing was welcoming. White bannisters, cream carpet, white emulsion on the walls. A large round window made it feel airy and light. Someone had trailed fairly lights at the foot of the bannisters, but they weren't glowing today, just several rows of plastic wire.

Ellie and Zoe followed Sylvia into the bedroom, where she pointed at the bed. The top of one bedside cabinet was empty except for a lamp. The other had moisturiser, novels, a phone charger. The duvet was folded back on this side. The other side looked unused. 'I've been next door,' Sylvia said. 'Owen's stuff is in there. They sleep in different rooms.'

'Way to go,' Zoe exclaimed. 'Stuff that bed sharing lark. Maybe he snores.'

'I know that one,' Ellie replied. 'I'd have loved a room to send your dad off to when he snored.'

'*And* ...' Sylvia said, 'seems Anna was reading up on caravans and motorhomes.'

Zoe swooped up the magazine. 'These are so cool. The Matthews have got one. Charlie and Finn are going to use it when they take the band on tour.'

But while Sylvia was chattering away about caravan holidays with Ron, there was something that Jaq had said that was scratching at the edges of Ellie's unconscious, which she was too tired to quite get a hold of. And she felt a growing sense of sadness that two of her friends, a couple, had been planning exciting holiday adventures and a new business – and now one of them had vanished into thin air.

'Right,' she said. 'We've seen enough here. Let's go home. I can't think straight – I need a kip.'

Chapter 11

It was 5pm by the time Ellie had finished her nap and Sylvia saw her shuffling downstairs to the kitchen in her fluffy, charcoal dressing gown, still a bit bleary-eyed.

'What is that deliciousness I can smell?' Ellie asked, inhaling deeply and heading straight for the oven.

There was a draught through an open window where the extension cable ran to the outhouse. Sylvia pulled the window closer to the frame and tried to lodge it in place on the plastic cable. She caught sight of Sarge and Sean through the open outhouse doors, helping with the laundry. Thank goodness, they'd taken all the bags and paraphernalia out there. She'd swept the floor, vacuumed, and was putting the mop over it when Ellie noticed.

'Aww. That's kind. Thank you. You can stay.' Ellie flicked the kettle on to boil. 'Cuppa?'

'Lovely, thanks. I've nearly finished.' Sylvia opened the oven and pulled a rack out.

'You know, I'm starting to share Anna's sense that something's happened to Owen.' Ellie followed Sylvia to the worktop, peering at her creations. 'Where is he? It's like he's disappeared in a puff of smoke.'

'It's not looking good, is it?'

The front door opened, and Zoe and Finn came in with another man, Finn's age. He was carrying a bag of tools and a longer extension cable on a reel.

When Zoe saw her mother, she gestured to her dressing gown and mouthed 'sorry' at her. 'This is Brian Douglas. He's going to sort the electricity for us. Given that's six electricians we've tried so far and haven't been able to get hold of.'

'Mrs Blix,' Brian said to Ellie, nodding his acknowledgement of her. 'Nice pumpkin lanterns out the front there.'

'I lit them,' said Sylvia. 'It's Halloween. That reminds me. I've got sweets for the children.' She took a bowl out of a cupboard and emptied a bumper pack of assorted confectionery into it.

'That's the salad bowl,' Ellie muttered.

Brian strode over to the worktop. 'Those smell good. What're you baking?' He reached to grab a rock bun and Sylvia play-slapped his hand away.

'Get out of it. You can have one *if* you fix our power.' She led Brian over to the fuse board.

He took one look at it and exclaimed in a loud voice, 'Good grief. I don't know how your electrics have lasted this long. This thing is positively medieval.'

'Oh fabulous,' Ellie called over. 'You're not going to scare us at all then.'

'Mu-um,' Zoe whispered. 'Be nice to him. He knows you and his mother don't get on, so he's come to help as a favour to Finn and me.' While the kettle was boiling, she parted her hair down the middle with her fingers and deftly plaited one side.

'Changing the subject – we *still* haven't had a team meeting yet,' said Sylvia. 'Don't you think we should? There's been rather a lot going on.'

'Good idea,' said Ellie.

'Give me a couple of minutes to finish this floor and I'll be with you. Rebus' muddy paws are a pain in the neck. Do you want to make tea for everyone, Zo, lovey?'

'Yeah, Gran.' She quickly plaited the other side of her hair and then took the milk carton out of the fridge.

Before they could start their meeting, there was a knock on the front door.

Rebus barked and shot over, squealing and wriggling.

'Dad's here,' shouted Zoe, having peered through the window.

Ellie tutted. 'Great. Another visitor.'

Sylvia suspected that Ellie felt like going back upstairs and getting into bed.

'Let him in, can you? I'm just getting rid of the mop.' She wondered if he was here in an official capacity, or a social one.

Dave, wearing a charcoal suit and brown suede brogues, followed Zoe into the kitchen.

'Oh,' he said, pointing at Ellie's attire. 'Suddenly, I feel a bit over-dressed.'

'One of us got about four hours' sleep last night,' she said in a monotone, giving Zoe the evil eye. 'To what do we owe this honour?'

'I need to ask you and Zoe some questions.' He peered over at Brian. '*Police questions.*'

'Don't mind me,' Brian said, his hand raised in submission. 'I'll be in the outhouse, checking the sockets, as soon as I've got my tea.' He winked at Zoe.

'Cheers, mate,' said Dave. He marched over to the cooling rack and snatched up a rock bun.

Brian shut the back door behind him.

Dave promptly locked it and took a bite of the warm, sweet bun. 'Isn't that Katie Douglas' son? I'm surprised you've even allowed him over the threshold.'

'I'm desperate,' Ellie replied.

He shrugged. 'I need to ask you both about seeing the hot air balloon. PC Smith passed on what Zoe told him at the search.'

'Oh, right, sure,' said Ellie. 'Are you investigating Owen's disappearance now?'

'Not exactly. Some new evidence has come to light, which I'm not able to share, I'm afraid. But I do need to ask you both some questions.'

'I'll just nip upstairs and get out of my dressing gown. Do you want to start with Zoe? I'll be a couple of minutes.'

'No problem.' He turned to Zoe.

Ellie made her way upstairs and Sylvia took over making the tea.

'How's it going?' He sat down at the table. 'Are you enjoying your new car?'

Zoe beamed at him. 'It's so cool.'

Sylvia brought over four mugs and placed them on the table with a jug of milk and some sugar. 'Do you know what's going on with these travelling gnomes? We've had one here and there was a different one at Anna's earlier too.'

'Only that someone's nicking them from the graveyard and people's houses.'

'Any idea who?'

'Something else I can't share, I'm afraid.' He turned to Zoe. 'OK. So – you told PC Smith you saw a hot air balloon around dawn on Saturday morning. Could you talk me through it, please?'

Zoe described it. Two people in silhouette. The balloon rising sharply.

'It wasn't too far away to get a good clear look at the basket?'

'I could see it perfectly. I took a picture.' She showed Dave the image on her phone.

'And when you said you'd seen *two* people, your mum said she'd seen *three*. Is that correct?'

'Yes.'

'Now, this might sound like a ridiculous question, but how do you explain the discrepancy?'

'Mum and I have talked about this. There aren't many options. Either one of us is wrong, or we both are. And I think Mum's wrong.'

'Go on.'

'We've come to the conclusion Mum must have been mistaken. Unless a third person was obscured in some way.'

Dave was nodding. 'And you said the balloon was rising. What did that look like?'

'It was shooting up in the air very fast and it was spinning and moving about.'

'Hmm. Interesting. Gust of wind maybe. Now, is there any way *you* could have been mistaken about there being two people in the basket?'

'No. I absolutely saw two. A man and a woman.'

'And when your mum said there were three, did that make you doubt what you saw?'

'No. I know what I saw. Mum either made a mistake or when she spotted them, there were three people in that basket.'

'You didn't see anyone fall?' he asked Zoe.

'No. Just the balloon rising sharply.'

'OK, that's all I need to ask you. I'll speak to your mum now.'

'Do you know what's happened to Owen Field?' asked Zoe.

Dave took a deep breath. 'I can't tell you anything, I'm afraid. You know that.'

'Are you investigating his disappearance? No-one's seen or heard from him for over a day and his car is at McDonald's.'

'We know that, and I'm afraid I cannot discuss with you what we are – and are not – investigating.'

'But you said new evidence has come to light? Is that about Owen?'

'I did, and it has, but I cannot divulge what it's in relation to. I'm sorry.'

Ellie was back now, in tracksuit bottoms and a hoodie. She joined them at the kitchen table, pulling her unruly brown hair into a top knot. 'Where are we?'

'*New evidence* has come to light apparently,' Zoe said, emphasising her first two words.

Sylvia brought over a teapot and placed it on the tray. A look passed between Ellie, Zoe and her.

'So I heard,' Ellie replied, looking at Dave. 'What new–'

'I can't share that, I'm afraid. *As you know.*'

Sylvia watched as Ellie chewed over what Dave had said and what it might mean. Despite their separation, she could see Ellie still understood Dave extremely well and was able to read him.

He put the same questions to Ellie as he had Zoe, pausing only to ask Ellie to focus on what she'd seen, compared to what Zoe saw.

'Again, this might sound strange but why did you think there were three people in the hot air balloon basket?'

'Because I *saw* three people. Or – at the time, I thought I did. Three separate individuals in the basket leaning towards each other as though they were raising a toast or joining hands or something like that.'

'Were you able to clearly make them all out?'

There was a knock at the door, followed by muted giggling.

Rebus shot over, barking.

'Of course,' said Ellie. 'It's Halloween.'

Sylvia grabbed up the bowl of sweets and opened the door.

'Trick or treat,' the children chorused excitedly.

'Hi, Mrs Blix,' one boy said.

Sylvia held out the bowl and the children swooped on it.

Charlie Matthews gave her a tired smile. 'Uncle duties. Only elleventy-billion more houses. How was your head this morning?' he asked, with a twinkle in his eye.

'Cheeky wretch. Absolutely fine. Congratulations on your gig. Most enjoyable.'

The children had got bored now and were already on their way to the house next door.

Sylvia said goodbye and returned to the table.

Ellie was answering Dave's question. 'At the time, I was sure I could see fine, but I had just woken up for the second time and might have been a bit sleepy still, and the sun was in my eyes.'

Dave smiled, as though he'd had a fleeting memory of how Ellie looked when she woke up. 'Is there any chance what you *thought* was the third person could have been an illusion? Or a trick of the light ... or, I don't know ... a shadow or something? Basically, is there any way you could have been mistaken?'

'I can't rule that out.'

'OK. Thank you, both.'

'Before you go, I was thinking about cooking a chilli tonight,' Zoe announced, looking at the clock on the kitchen wall. 'Do you want to come for supper, Dad?'

'Oh. That's news to me,' said Ellie.

'Sorry, Mum. Finn and I were talking about it earlier and he nipped to the butcher's to get some mince. Hadn't got round to mentioning it. It's cool though, right? With potato wedges and sour cream? Otherwise we can freeze the mince.'

'Sure.' Ellie knew Zoe and Finn were up to something but was too tired to kick up a fuss. 'Saves me cooking.'

'I don't like chilli,' said Sylvia. 'Sets off my acid reflux.'

'We'll make you your own special mild pot, Gran. Don't worry. With a sprinkle of paprika only.'

Dave glanced from Zoe to his mum and then Ellie, and Sylvia caught a wistful look on her son's face, as though he missed the family banter. 'I suspect we've just been Zoe-ed … but I'd love to. Saves me from having yet another toasted ham and cheese sandwich when I get in from work.'

Zoe beamed and went over to her dad, sliding her arm round his shoulders and putting her face close to his. 'Love you, Dad.'

He shifted his head so he could kiss her forehead. 'You too, daughter.' He moved a little and Zoe let go of him. 'Right. Better get back to the office. I'll be back in an hour or so to eat.' He paused, as though there was something else he wanted to say. 'By the way, I've been offered a promotion. It's setting up a new unit. A challenge.'

'That's great. Congratulations.' Ellie knew suitable and appealing positions didn't come up often. 'Doing what?'

'I'll tell you more later. The thing is…' A nervous look flashed across his face, '… it's not in Kent.'

A sense of foreboding swept over Ellie. 'Where is it?'

'The Midlands.'

Chapter 12

'A missing person's case,' Ellie announced. 'Are we ready for this, team?'

She, Sylvia and Zoe were in the kitchen, sitting round the table, finally having their first meeting.

'I can't believe you haven't said anything about Dad moving away,' Zoe blurted out, her cheeks growing blotchier by the second.

'Oh, lovey.' Ellie sighed. 'He's just considering it at the moment.'

'Yeah, but what if he goes?' Zoe's tone was a panicky screech.

'Perhaps he wants a fresh start. He's been at Kent Police all his career.'

'But what about you and him? How are you two going to get back together if he's in the stoopid Midlands? He might meet someone.'

Ellie heaved in a breath and tried to let Zoe's comments wash over her, but the idea of Dave with someone else stirred up the memories of his affair. She opened her notepad. 'It's his choice, Zo.'

'Because he thinks you don't love him.'

Sylvia sucked in air through pursed lips and held her breath.

'That isn't true – or fair. I've been very clear with him about how I feel.' Ellie tucked a curl behind her ear. 'Anyway – we'll be able to talk to him more about it over the chilli you and Finn are cooking.'

'Suppose.' Zoe drummed her fingers on the table, face mutinous.

'Shall we talk about Owen now?' Ellie asked gently.

Zoe twiddled her plaits. 'Does any of us really think this is a missing person case? What does it even mean to say someone's gone missing? It just means it's not known where the person is, surely? They haven't been found and could be dead or alive.'

'Yes, it's a bit of a catch-all term, isn't it?' said Sylvia.

'Anna is convinced "something has happened",' Ellie continued. 'And, although she hasn't spelled it out, it's pretty obvious she thinks he's come to harm.'

'His brother, by the sound of it, thinks he went to McDonald's to meet someone.' Sylvia raised her eyebrows. 'And then what?'

'And you and I wondered,' said Zoe to her gran, 'if he could have gone walking and had an accident. Fallen into the marsh or slipped off the cliffs.'

'Yes. And something none of us have mentioned so far, because we don't want to worry Anna,' said Sylvia, 'is whether he's left his life here, either for a new one elsewhere or whether – God forbid – he's taken his life.'

Ellie nodded. 'That's the mystery. Where did he go after he left Anna on Saturday morning? What happened and where is he now?' She took the lid off her biro and jotted down those three questions. 'Shall we look at what doesn't currently stack up?'

Sylvia cleared her throat. 'The most obvious thing is why Owen would get up at 5am and drive to his brother's for a hot air balloon ride, only to decide, on the way there, he's not going after all.'

'Unless he'd wanted to cancel before that,' said Zoe, 'and for some reason hadn't done so, but in the car realised he couldn't go.' She looked first at her mum then her grandmother. 'You know how sometimes you put off telling a person you don't fancy doing something because you don't want to hurt their feelings or cause a row...?'

They both nodded.

'But the depth of feeling remains,' she continued, 'or even increases, and then you get into a panic because you haven't said anything, and it all comes out at the last minute.'

'Oh, I hate that,' said Sylvia. 'We've all done it. Yes, I can see how that might work. Perhaps Owen didn't want to spoil things because it was John and Gail's wedding anniversary, so he tried to push his feelings down to make it possible for himself to go.'

Ellie and Zoe nodded.

'Alternatively,' Sylvia continued, 'it's possible that none of that was going on. Perhaps he *did* want to go but – as John suggests – something happened on the way or when he got there. After all, we only have his brother's word for it that Owen changed his mind about going on the ride while he was driving to meet them.'

Zoe raised one hand in an exaggerated 'stop' gesture. 'OK. That now introduces the brother. What do we make of John?'

'I only know Owen a bit from the pub,' said Sylvia, 'but he and his brother seem quite different. The other day, I'd ordered a steak there when I was having lunch with the vicar–'

'Are you and the Reverend an item, Gran? That's twice now you've been out with him.'

'Reverend Jackson and I are *friends*, thank you,' she said, being careful to emphasise the word.

'If you say so,' Zoe muttered.

Sylvia bristled. 'I do. He's looking after St Mary's for a month while–'

'We know.' Zoe tapped the side of her nose, deliberately trying to wind up her gran.

'My crystal ball tells me that – one way or another – we're going to be seeing a lot more of the vicar,' said Ellie as she winked at Zoe.

Sylvia tutted loudly. 'As I was saying – I was in the pub, and I asked for my steak to be *properly* cooked. I don't like any pinkness, let alone blood.' She shuddered. 'And chefs are often reluctant to cook it that way because they think it will make it tough and you'll complain.'

'*And* because they think they know best,' said Zoe.

'That too sometimes,' Sylvia continued. 'But I explained it all to the waitress and Owen was so good about it. He came out and asked me how well-cooked I wanted it, and said he completely understood that a lot of people don't like pink meat. His brother, in contrast, seems much brasher. What did you think of him, Zoe?'

'Hmm. He's very alpha male, isn't he? Comfortable issuing orders too. I even wondered at one point whether he'd been in the military. But I put it down to him being extremely concerned about finding his brother.'

'Sometimes men who've had high-powered jobs can get like that,' said Ellie.

'Bossy, you mean?' said Sylvia. 'He wants to keep everyone safe. But I agree. There's no doubt he wants to find Owen. I assume he's the older brother, is he?'

'I don't know,' Ellie replied.

'I got the impression he was prepared to search every centimetre of ground to find him.'

'I wasn't there and haven't met him yet,' said Ellie, 'but I wonder if there was conflict between the two brothers over the pub. Owen has worked there for a long time. It seems like his brother has swanned in and taken over as manager. It might be useful to have a chat with the bar staff. See what the word is on the ground. Anna mentioned someone called Trudy.'

'She used to go out with Charlie Matthews,' said Zoe. 'I worked with her when I was there. She's cool.'

Ellie gave Zoe a thumbs up and jotted the name on her notepad. 'It would be useful to verify John's account and that the other person on the balloon ride was his wife.'

Zoe swiped her phone and tapped at the screen. 'The Windmill Inn. Managers,' she said aloud as she scrolled. 'John and Gail Field.'

'Well done. If Gail's up for it, let's see if we can have a chat with her in the morning. Once I've made sure that Sarge and his nephew are on top of the laundry situation, I'll be good to go.' She added Gail's name to her list. 'We've talked about the relationship between the two brothers. What about Owen and Anna's relationship? Anna's sister, Jaq, said they're happy and good friends. Any comments or observations?'

Sylvia took a breath. 'You know, I've often heard it said that one person in a relationship always loves the other more. If we had to think about Owen and Anna in those terms, who would you say loved the other person most?'

'Owen,' the three of them choroused.

'Interesting that we've all got that impression. Where's it come from?' Ellie found herself reflecting on the picture she'd built up of her yoga teacher friend over the years. Had she got the sense from Anna that she was happy in her marriage? In her life? Ellie wasn't sure. She knew Anna's yoga teaching was important to her and that she found it fulfilling, but she'd always got the sense something was ... what? Lacking? She couldn't quite put her finger on it. Or maybe that was just the reality of adult life.

'When Dave and I have been round there for dinner, Owen has always done the cooking while Anna did the entertaining. I understand he's a chef, but when you have guests round as a couple you want to share the work so that both of you can enjoy the evening. Often Dave would feel sorry for Owen and go and chat to him in the kitchen, and Anna and I would chat round the table. It felt a bit pointless us being there because until we sat down to eat, we weren't all able to talk.'

'And your point is?' asked Zoe jokingly, as she strummed her fingers on the table.

'It felt like he was waiting on her. As if he saw his role as subservient to her. Plus, he would often gaze at her adoringly whereas I don't think I've seen her doing that to him.'

'When Finn was doing the log deliveries a couple of weeks ago,' said Zoe, 'he dropped some off at their place. Anna wasn't there. It was in the morning and I think she was out teaching. Owen was about to go to work. When Finn asked him where he wanted the logs, he mentioned where Anna likes them to go and that she likes a certain amount to be inside, drying, and the rest outside in the log store.'

'OK, so we think Anna's the boss and Owen is more in love with her than she is with him. What does that mean? Anything?'

'I don't know. You brought it up, Gran.'

'I don't think it means anything at the moment, but it's good to know what some of the dynamics are in their relationship because these are bound to have had an effect on both of them. Something I mentioned earlier but we haven't discussed yet is whether or not it's possible that Owen might have taken his own life. What do we think about that?'

'Oh, goodness. I really hope not. Do you think that's what's happened?' Zoe stared at her grandmother in horror.

'I have no idea but it's something we need to consider as an option because it's one of a few outcomes of people going missing. Along with whether he might have left Anna for a life elsewhere, or to be with someone else.'

'Sylvia's right about those being possible consequences,' Ellie added.

Zoe shook her head. 'That doesn't fit with him adoring her, though, and leaving her love notes.'

'Unless he found that dynamic hard,' Sylvia explained. 'Some people don't mind being the partner who loves the other more. My Ron always used to say he loved me more than I loved him.'

Ellie and Zoe waited to hear what she was going to say.

'It's often about perception. I never saw it that way. If anything, I would have put it the other way round. But whichever it was, I certainly appreciated his love. And, luckily, it didn't bother him. He knew I'd not had an easy time with Mum and that it had affected me.'

'That's so romantic,' said Zoe, her expression soft. 'Who do you think loves who most, Mum? You or Dad?'

'Oh, er ... I have no idea.' Ellie felt a twist of irritation but wanted to be patient with Zoe. She knew how desperate she was for her parents to get back together. 'You've used the present tense there. We're separated, don't forget.'

'Yeah, but you still love each other.'

Ellie blushed and then felt momentarily embarrassed.

Sylvia leaned over to Zoe and said gently, 'A few minutes ago you were accusing her of not loving your dad.'

'No, I wasn't. I said that Dad *thinks* she doesn't love him.'

'And we established that isn't true either,' said Ellie. She felt like she was being forced to admit to a crush on someone at school.

Sylvia stepped in. 'It's not really about romance. It's the reality of a lot of long-term partnerships. I read about it when I was a social worker as I wanted to understand the relationship choices my clients made.' She paused. 'They matter, because they lie beneath so many of our problems in life.'

The phrase struck Ellie. How true it was.

'And?' said Zoe.

'Unconsciously, we pick partners who fulfil a particular role, depending on our experiences growing up.'

'How can we do it unconsciously?'

'Who we're attracted to isn't always something we're aware of. We often don't think about why we like certain types of people and with certain traits.' She gave a quick smile.

Zoe slumped in her chair. 'I liked Finn for years before we got together. Never breathed a word. He knows about it now though.'

Ellie slipped her arm round Zoe's shoulders. When she'd found out Zoe and Finn were seeing each other, she had been worried about Finn's anger towards his mother. Fortunately, that had settled down.

'He's a lovely young man,' said Sylvia. 'Luckily, I chose a good man too. Or – he chose me.' She gathered her breath. 'But, for others, it can be painful to love another person more.'

'Why though?' asked Zoe.

'It can make them feel vulnerable and scared. For example, I had a young client at work who always felt she loved her boyfriends more than they loved her. It was an extremely destructive dynamic, and made her suspicious and excessively watchful because she was constantly expecting them to leave her or cheat on her.'

'That's so sad.' Zoe looked traumatised. 'Gran, I love your social work stories and experience. You've had such an amazing life. You're like an encyclopaedia.'

'That wasn't what you said earlier.' Sylvia adopted a mock-serious tone. 'You said I was like a financial adviser.'

'Sorry, I was being an idiot.'

Ellie felt a warm rush of love for the two very different women who surrounded her every day. Sylvia, in many ways so wise. Zoe, all youthful expressiveness and naivety. 'This brings us to the possibility we mentioned – Owen's had some sort of an accident and is laid up somewhere.'

'And can't call home?' Zoe asked.

'I agree, that is strange, unless he's incapacitated.' Ellie tapped her pen on her pad, chewing over options. She found it hard not to imagine him up to his neck in the marsh, or flat out on the rocks at the bottom of the chalk cliffs down to Dover.

'Anna said his phone goes straight to voicemail so perhaps the battery is flat,' suggested Zoe.

'Yes, that's possible too,' Ellie replied. 'I think all we can do for now is bear in mind what we started with, which is that we don't know yet whether Owen is alive somewhere or dead. Shall we make a list of who we need to speak to tomorrow?'

'Trudy and some of the bar staff at the Windmill Inn,' said Zoe. 'And John's wife, Gail.'

Sylvia was rubbing her chin. 'I'd like to speak to John properly. I was only able to ask him one question at the search. There are several others I'd like to put to him.'

'It's interesting the police have assessed Owen as being a low risk missing person,' said Ellie, thinking back to their earlier point. 'Presumably that means they don't think he's taken his own life. Which is a relief.'

'Yes, but they can only form their assessment on the basis of the information that's available to them,' Sylvia added. 'What if things have been going on that the police don't know about? Like financial or health problems. I think it's worth asking Anna a few more questions. Don't you?'

'Was John's wife at either of the searches, did either of you notice?' Ellie asked. 'I didn't see.'

'I don't know what she looks like so I can't answer that,' said Zoe.

'Same here,' said Sylvia. 'When we joined the search John was leading, it was already underway, so it wasn't like people were standing around chatting, introducing each other and so on.'

'Well, it won't be hard to find her,' said Ellie. 'Presumably, she'll be either at the pub or at their place in Eythorne. I would like to know whether she was helping to search for her brother-in-law. And to find out how they got on.'

'Before we finish,' said Zoe, 'I've been chewing a couple of things over. The first is whether anyone else in the village saw John and Gail's hot air balloon on Saturday morning. The second is whether anyone local has experience of flying balloons.'

'Go on,' said Sylvia.

'Regarding the balloon: they took off before sunrise and landed afterwards. There must have been other people who saw it. They're massive, and that one was a deep orangey-red. You can't miss it.'

'I agree,' said Ellie.

'I'm thinking of shift workers, dog walkers, fishermen, joggers, postmen, delivery drivers ...'

'Lots of people would have been getting up for work,' said Ellie. 'Any of them could have seen the balloon and could verify whether there were two or three people in the basket.'

'What do you think about me asking for information on Facebook?' asked Zoe.

'It's a great idea potentially – but the Lower Wootton Facebook page is public,' said Sylvia, 'so if you post asking if anyone saw the balloon, and there has been criminal activity, anyone replying could make themselves vulnerable. And it could interfere with the police investigation.'

'Or they could deliberately give false information.'

'That too. I would suggest not doing it publicly. Let's see if we can think of other ways of getting that information without doing it in such an obvious way.'

'I agree,' said Ellie. 'It's a great idea though, Zo, lovey.'

'What about Facebook groups for dog-walkers and joggers?' asked Zoe. 'They're likely to be private.'

'That's different,' Sylvia replied. 'If Owen has been harmed, it's very unlikely that the perpetrator is going to go looking in dog-walking groups for people with incriminating information.'

'Well done,' said Ellie. 'Posting in them could yield some useful evidence. Let us know what you find out, will you?'

Chapter 13

Rebus heard Dave arrive long before Ellie. He shot to the door, his claws clacking on the floorboards. Finn and Zoe were in the kitchen, tasting the chilli and basting the potato wedges they'd put in the oven.

Ellie let Dave in and Agatha-the-cockerpoo hurled herself at her legs, almost knocking her over.

'I'm dog-sitting while Simon and Jen are away,' said Dave. 'Hope you don't mind me bringing her. Forgot to mention it earlier.'

Simon was Zoe's older brother.

The two dogs tore round the ground floor of the windmill, squealing and somersaulting, a wriggling mass of golden curls.

Dave must have nipped home to change, as the suit had been replaced by grey jeans and a cotton shirt. He handed her a bottle of wine and gave her a peck on the cheek.

'Smells good. My cholesterol will appreciate a break from greasy toasties.' He grinned at Ellie and followed her in.

'Hey, Dad. The food will be about twenty minutes, you two. Do you want to go and sit in the lounge? We'll bring you through a drink. What would you like?'

'Your dad's brought some wine. Shall we have that?'

Dave nudged Ellie. 'Do they want something or have they done something? I'm getting the distinct impression there's some sucking-up going on here.'

Sylvia joined them from the office. 'Evening.' She sidled over to Zoe and peered over her shoulder at the food.

'Mum,' said Dave warmly.

'I'd love a glass of wine, if one's going,' said Sylvia.

'As I was saying... The sucking-up?'

Finn chuckled. 'Nothing like that, Mr Blix.' He flicked a tea towel over his shoulder. 'Just helping out a bit. And we haven't seen you for a while so we thought it would be nice to invite you round for supper.'

Sylvia, who was still hovering, was taking in the exchange.

'In that case, I should be grateful. Thank you. No alcohol for me though, please. I'm on call. A soft drink would be lovely.' He turned to Ellie. 'Let's go and sit down then, shall we?' He took his coat and scarf off and hung them up on the hooks by the door.

Ellie was thinking about Finn's comment. It was true. It was a long time since Dave had been over for supper. In fact, she couldn't remember when the last time was. She wondered how he felt about being a guest in his old home. She wasn't sure how *she* felt about it. And she hadn't deliberately *not* invited him over. It was simply that the days seemed to whizz by, taken up with Blix Blitz work and the day-to-day business of life and being a mum.

Dave went over to the music centre and switched it on. 'Fancy some tunes?' He scoured the room for the CD towers, frowning slightly. 'My music's gone.' He looked a bit hurt.

Ellie squirmed momentarily. 'We put the CDs in the outhouse to create some space. Zoe and Finn don't listen to Pink Floyd and Led Zeppelin. And they stream music straight from their phones. Sylvia listens mainly to the radio and podcasts, and I don't have time to listen to anything these days.'

'Oh. Right.' He rubbed his chin. 'Of course. I'll take them back to mine then at some point. Spotify?' He swiped at his phone. 'I can't seem to find the Wi-Fi. It's the one beginning SKY586P, isn't it? It's not coming up for some reason.'

'We changed provider. Zoe used a comparison website and we managed to get a cheaper deal.'

'No worries. I'll use the data on my phone.' He selected a playlist and the music began.

'Are you investigating Owen's disappearance?' Ellie asked.

Finn arrived with wine for Ellie and a Coke for Dave. 'Here you go.' He handed the drinks over.

'Thank you,' she said.

'Cheers, buddy. That's very kind.' He turned to Ellie. 'Uniform are making enquiries, I believe. Not CID.'

Ellie wanted to tread carefully. She was aware it had caused problems between her and Dave in the past when she quizzed him about investigations. 'Can I ask you about that then?'

His expression tightened. 'That depends. Fire away and I'll soon say what I can't tell you.' He sat down on the sofa.

'Where do you think Owen is?'

'I don't know but I'm not familiar with all the details.'

'Anna thinks something's happened to him. She's asked us to help find him.'

'Ah. I see. Well, at least you told me this time.' He took a sip of Coke. 'Do you think he could have left her?'

'It's crossed my mind and I'm sure it has hers too. But he's a decent bloke. Why would he do it like that? And why would he leave his car at McDonald's? I mean, if you wanted to leave, surely you'd take the car?'

'Does she have her own vehicle?'

'Yes.'

He shrugged. 'Maybe he doesn't need it where he's gone to.'

'Yeah, but if he wanted to separate, why not say so?'

'It can be hard. He wouldn't be the first person to leave a partner that way.' He paused. 'Sometimes it's hard to … to …,' he stammered, unusually for him. 'Hard to say you're …'

Of course. He was talking about his brief affair with Finn's mother, Andrea. 'Not happy?'

Dave blushed. 'Sometimes, yes. In my case, it wasn't quite that. You know – we talked about it.'

For Ellie, her conversations with Dave about why he had started an affair were etched on the folds of her brain. In some ways she wished she could forget them. In others, she was pleased she couldn't. But she was reminded of Zoe's comments earlier. She was about to broach the subject when Dave said, 'Why does Anna think something's happened?'

'No one thing in particular. Just that lots of details don't add up, and it's not like him.'

'Hmm. Not sure what I can say really.' He sipped his Coke. 'She knows him better than anyone. But often there are things about people's lives even their nearest and dearest don't know.'

'She said he's been assessed as a low risk missing person. Is that right?'

'I believe so. But those assessments are only as accurate as the information the police have access to. If there's stuff they don't know about ...' His sentence tailed off. 'It's not an exact science, I'm afraid.'

That confirmed what the three of them had discussed earlier at their meeting.

'His brother is doing land searches with groups of volunteers.'

Dave nodded. 'Yes, I heard. Let's hope he turns up. Nice fella, Owen. Changing the subject ...' He dropped his voice. 'What's the latest with Mum? Is she still planning to move out or has she changed her mind?'

'She's still deciding. Now she's sold her house, she's a free agent. I think she's considering her options. She seems to have struck up a friendship with the vicar from Harbledown.'

'Ah, yes. Reverend Jackson. He was in touch with me about some scallywag nicking a gnome off one of the graves at the church. Passed him onto uniform.'

They chatted about the travelling gnome phase and the gnome he'd seen outside the windmill when he'd come round on Saturday morning.

'I saw Mum and the vicar in the pub the other night.' He smiled. 'It's good to see her happy. She must miss Dad terribly. They were soulmates.'

'Actually, she's been much more content since the summer when she got back in contact with her mother.'

'Yes, that was one of a few good things that came out of those tragic murders.' He chuckled. 'Mary's an amazing woman, Ells. And it's definitely helped with my relationship with Mum to know more about what went on.' He looked in the direction of the kitchen. 'I could never understand why she was dead set against me joining the police.'

Ellie smiled. 'How is Mary's police antipathy going?'

'She's slowly warming up.' He looked round the room. 'Anyway, enough about them. How are you?'

'Ticking along, I guess. Zoe and Finn are looking forward to Christmas and–'

'And you?' He looked at her directly now.

'Christmas hasn't been my favourite time for a while.'

It had been at Christmas two years earlier that Ellie had learned of Dave's affair.

'Where are we with all that?'

'*We?*'

'Well – *you*. I know where I am. I want us to get back together.'

'Sad,' she said quickly. 'Very sad, is where I am.'

'Me too.' He paused. 'Shall we do a family Christmas here? With Simon and Jen, if they're around. Mary too?'

The idea warmed Ellie. 'Why not?'

'Are you going to the fireworks?'

'Yes.'

'Shall we go together?' Dave spoke gently, as though he was nervous to ask.

'Er ...' This was two suggestions in a row. 'Yes. That'd be nice. Zoe and Finn are–' She broke off. 'Or did you mean ... like a date?'

'Would that be horrendous?' Dave blushed and fidgeted in his seat.

Ellie felt a flutter in her tummy. 'No, no. Not at all. I just ...' She paused. 'You know what? I'm so tired from the ruddy foxes waking me up at night. I can hardly think straight. But – yes. Why not?' The thought of it simultaneously filled her with excitement and fear. But it was OK. They were hardly going to be alone with a hundred or so locals on the village green.

'Speaking of people moving, what's this new post you're considering in the Midlands?' Ellie's stomach lurched as she asked the question. Like her, Dave had been born in Lower Wootton and the place wouldn't be the same without him.

'It's taking the lead on something I've wanted to do for a long time. An inner-city project in Birmingham, aiming to tackle violence against women and girls–'

Dave's phone vibrated. He slid it out of his jacket. 'DI Blix.' He listened. 'Hold on a minute, mate, could you?' He turned to Ellie. 'Excuse me.'

Ellie watched Dave's face as he listened.

'OK,' he said. 'The gun's gone too, has it? I'll be five minutes.' He faced Ellie, his face serious. 'Sorry. Could we take a rain check on that conversation? I've got to go.' He stood up. 'Can you hang onto Agatha?'

Chapter 14
SUNDAY

W hen Ellie got downstairs the next morning, the house was deserted. There was no sign of Zoe and Finn, or Rebus. They must've taken him out for a walk. And Sylvia left at 8am on Sundays for bell-ringing at the church.

After another night of broken sleep, partly due to the foxes again, she had the beginnings of a headache. Dave had been on her mind constantly. It was all very well saying she felt fine about him potentially taking up a job in Birmingham, but she knew from the pull in her stomach that she hoped he wouldn't go.

It wasn't Scotland, thankfully. But it *was* two hundred miles away, and that would add a geographical separation to their marital one. No bumping into each other in the pub or the fish and chip shop. No passing Rebus and Agatha back and forth for dog care and walks. No coming home and finding him mending Zoe's bike over a beer with Finn. It felt like another step in a direction she didn't want. At the same time, though, it felt unfair to impose *her* wishes onto him. Especially since she still wasn't able to agree to getting back together.

She had a quick shower, got dressed and had breakfast. Zoe had left a note prompting Ellie to ask Gail Field if their doorbell video was connected.

When Ellie got round to the Windmill Inn, she was relieved to learn Gail was there. She nipped up the stairs to the front room, above the main bar. Gail was leaning over removal boxes. She had an athletic frame and her sportswear suggested she'd either just got home from the gym or had done a home workout. She had no make-up on, and her skin was shiny from moisturiser.

'Really sorry about your brother-in-law's disappearance,' said Ellie. Her temples were aching and her mouth was dry. 'It must be a very worrying time for you.'

'Thank you. It is. I do hope nothing's happened to him.' She gestured to the boxes. 'We were looking forward to living here at the pub, but somehow I don't feel remotely like unpacking.' She was placing ornaments at intervals around the room. From a cardboard box, she pulled out a photograph frame, dusted the glass with a cloth and placed it on a shelf next to the fireplace. It was one of her and John, both smiling, their arms round each other's waists. 'Still – at least it keeps my mind occupied.'

'That's a lovely shot of the two of you,' Ellie said.

They made a handsome couple. Well-matched physically, a similar height and physique, both fit and active.

'Have you both always been sporty?'

'Yes. Actually, John and I met flying hot air balloons.'

'Oh, nice. Where?'

'I used to be part of a group and would crew for whoever needed help. It was a good way of getting experience and meeting people. John needed someone for a competition one day as he'd been let down. I knew a bit more than just how to inflate a balloon. We won the cup.'

'Wow. Obviously a successful partnership.' Ellie couldn't help thinking there was a reason why Gail was telling her this story.

'Seems like a lifetime ago now though.' She gave a small, rather sad, smile.

Ellie changed tack. 'I suppose your anniversary must have been marred by Owen's disappearance?'

'Well, yes. I hope we don't look heartless going up in our balloon when Owen's … wherever he is.'

Ellie frowned.

'We never thought anything of it when he texted, saying he wasn't coming–'

'Was that how he let you know he'd changed his mind? By text?'

She nodded. 'We thought a meeting had come up and he'd decided to do that instead. It's happened quite a lot recently.'

Ellie was thinking about this and wondered about the meetings Owen was apparently having.

'If John hadn't wanted to go up in the balloon still, I wouldn't have minded at all. I'd happily have gone back home. It was meant to be a family celeb–' She didn't finish her sentence.

'Oh, I understand completely.' Ellie noticed Gail said Owen had texted, whereas John told Sylvia he'd rung from the car. 'These occasions are special, aren't they? Family events. If one person is missing, it ruins it for everyone.'

Ellie felt a bit of a cow for being disingenuous. It wasn't as though she didn't believe what she was saying. Family *was* important to her. But she was saying it in order to encourage John's wife to open up and therefore wasn't being completely straightforward with her.

'Did you do the full trip?' Ellie had never been in a hot air balloon before, so she didn't know anything about how they worked. 'The route you'd planned, I mean.'

'It's not really like that,' replied Gail, as she placed two large candle holders on either side of the fireplace. 'When you go up in a balloon, you're at the mercy of the wind. You get blown where the wind wants you to go and the only controls you have are up and down. Bit of a simplification but pretty much true.'

Ellie gulped. 'Gosh, I think I'd find that rather terrifying. How do you arrange for someone to come and meet you to help you pack the balloon away?'

'Generally, you get an idea from the wind direction and speed, and you have someone on standby in a vehicle, and then when you're closer to the ground you call them and let them know where you'll be landing, so they can meet you.'

'Is that what you did? Had someone come and meet you?'

'Yes. Nice chap. George. George Oaks. He's worked for John for years at our old pub.'

'Think we met him on the search yesterday.'

'I leave John to arrange the crew though. I just go up for the ride and the champagne these days.' She blushed and returned to her boxes.

'It must be nice having some of your Canterbury staff work here at the Windmill. Saves trying out new people.'

Ellie couldn't help thinking about some of the cleaners she'd hired. It was such a relief when things clicked.

'Yes, he's our head barman. Very good cook too, as it happens.'

'Did he help Owen in the kitchen?'

'No. He was itching to, though. Had lots of ideas for new dishes; menus to try.'

'Was Owen open to these?'

She shook her head. 'George didn't have any training and Owen is old school; likes things done properly.' She said it as though it was a bad thing.

Ellie sensed tension. 'Did that cause a problem?'

'A bit, I think. The pub game isn't well-paid and it's long, late hours with minimal holidays. Most staff are looking for any promotions they can get.'

They hadn't spoken to George yet and Ellie made a mental note to ask him about this aspect of his job.

As Gail had been talking, Ellie had been trying to decide whether or not to mention that she and Zoe had seen the balloon. It was an opportunity that was too good to miss.

'My daughter and I saw your balloon from the windmill.'

'Oh, that's right, you and your family live next door in that lovely building, don't you? You've got the advantage there of the most amazing views. Could you see us clearly?

It's such a pretty balloon. The canvas is a deep, burnt orange.'

'Actually, we both saw you at different time intervals.' She told Gail what they'd seen. 'We can't quite decide which of us was imagining things.' She gave a little laugh, feeling another tug in her tummy.

'Well, sorry to tell you, your daughter got it right. It was just John and me ... but it's very hard to tell from that distance, isn't it? I don't know if you wear glasses, but I can't see a thing these days without my varifocals.' She gave an exaggerated eye-roll. 'The joys of old age.'

Ellie was pretty sure that Gail was younger than her and Gail wasn't wearing her trusty glasses in the lounge. But – never mind, she was right about the eyesight. Ellie had meant to go and get her eyes checked for ages now. Never seemed to have the time, or she'd book an appointment and something would come up.

'I'm sure you're right. Can't say I'm looking forward to telling Zoe though. That's my daughter. She was adamant she saw only two people. She'll be bragging for weeks.' She gathered her thoughts. 'Oh well. I was imagining things. At least I know now.'

Ellie was curious to know how Gail and John were enjoying their move. 'How are you settling in? I gather you're not actually living in Wootton yet. I hope, with your husband running the pub, you feel part of the village?'

'Oh, very much, we love it here. And now we've bought the pub, we'll be selling the house in Eythorne or renting it out so we can be live-in landlords. That's what John's always wanted. His own pub.'

Wait. Did she say they'd bought the Windmill Inn?

Finn and Anna had said John was *managing* it, hadn't they? They mustn't know about this development.

But mention of the house had reminded Ellie about Zoe's note. 'While I think of it, is your video doorbell connected at The Vines?'

'Yes. John is fastidious about security. It's linked to both our phones. Why do you ask?'

Ellie explained about the travelling gnomes. 'There was one outside your house. The same one as was outside our place next door.'

'How very odd. And rather sinister, don't you think?'

'I do. Stealing them isn't nice. Nor is it kind to taunt the owners with pictures. But I'm interested in why certain people in the village are being targeted.' She told Gail about Mr Blackman's grave. 'It would be useful to have a look at your app, if you wouldn't mind. See who's doing it.'

'Of course. How upsetting for his wife.'

'Yes. Thank you. I'm not very good with technology so I'll get my daughter to pop over. Take a look.' She changed the subject back to the pub. 'Speaking of Zoe, I think her boyfriend is going to be doing a gig for you at some point, with his band The Barn Owls. He said he'd arranged it with the new manager. I didn't know you'd bought the place. Congratulations.'

'Thank you.' She smiled warmly. 'It's a very recent thing and was the next step up for us, really. We'd managed the pub in Canterbury for several years and wanted to be our own bosses. The Windmill Inn is such an iconic building, and we love the village. A cathedral city is glamorous but there's nothing like a busy village pub, is there?' She seemed energised now. 'I've never known a pub with so much going on. Book club. A writing group. Folk Night. Quiz. Wootton Yarners. Weight Watchers...'

'We're all very fond of this place,' Ellie told her. But she was thinking about Owen. 'How did your brother-in-law feel about you buying the pub?'

Her face tensed up. 'We were disappointed he didn't want to go into partnership with us, but we respected his decision. He's got plans of his own.'

A confused frown flashed across Ellie's face. 'I'm not with you. Anna said Owen *wanted* to buy a share.' And then there was the draft contract for the Rattling Cat.

Gail shook her head. 'Unfortunately not. As I said, that was what *we* wanted. It was a shame. Would've been nice for John and Owen to be partners. We ended up buying the place on our own.'

'How strange. Perhaps I misheard her?'

'Anna's very busy with her yoga practice and her own life. She might have got it wrong. I don't know.' She paused, looking at another photograph of herself and John, this time holding up a medal, an inflated hot air balloon behind them.

'So, there was no bad feeling about you and your husband buying this place?'

'No. None at all. Owen adores the pub and he's a brilliant chef. I'm sure he'll back in the kitchen very soon.'

And as Gail spoke, Ellie realised there was a lot more she needed to know about Owen's aspirations, and how he felt about now working *for* his brother.

Chapter 15

After bell-ringing, Sylvia decided to make a new batch of shortbread before she left to talk to Trudy, the barmaid. She didn't usually put chocolate chips in her mixture, but her mother had recently given her a recipe to try.

She ripped the packet open and got a whiff of the lovely rich, Belgian chocolate. The recipe said to add 80g of chocolate chips, so she scattered in half the 200g packet and folded them into the mixture. Finn was in charge of taking the finished items out of the oven.

Zoe and Finn were both sitting at the kitchen table with their laptops in front of them, looking up useful Facebook groups to ask questions in. Next to a large vase of roses, Mouse, Finn's cat, was sitting licking his paws and cleaning his ears.

Sylvia's phone pinged on the table.

Zoe peered at the lock screen. 'Message from Mum. "Gail said–" I can't read the rest. It's chopped off.'

'Bring it over, lovey, can you?' She wiped her fingers on a cloth and took the phone from Zoe, then read Ellie's text message aloud.

'Gail said she and John have BOUGHT the pub. Owen texted John, not phoned. The crew person is George Oaks. Will speak to G now.'

'I know George,' Finn piped up. 'He was in my year at school. He came to our gig on Friday night. He's big into cooking, if I remember correctly. His nickname at school was Pudding.'

'He led one of the searches yesterday,' Sylvia said. She hit reply on Ellie's text. *'Did George want to cook at pub – conflict with Owen?'*

With these developments, she was impatient now to see what John had to say. If he and his wife had bought the pub from under Owen's nose, that could've caused bad feeling between them. 'OK to leave in about ten minutes?' she said to Zoe.

Zoe gave her a thumbs up. 'I've found a running group. How about this? "Were you out jogging ...?" No, they don't like that word ... "Were you out *running* in the Wootton area early Saturday morning around 6.30am to 7am? If so, please get in touch."'

'Perfect. Do we need to say what for?' asked Finn.

'It's tricky, isn't it?' replied Zoe. 'If we say we're looking for people who saw a hot air balloon, it's more specific, but could alert the wrong people.' She twiddled her hair. 'And, given Anna mentioned on Facebook that Owen was last seen heading off for a hot air balloon ride, it might put people off from getting in touch if they think they're going to get mixed up in a missing person's case.'

'On the other hand,' said Finn, 'it might make some people *more* inclined to reply if they know Owen and want to help.'

'True.' Zoe pursed her lips. 'We could try posting in one group without mentioning the balloon and in another group mention it. See which gets the best response.'

'That's a great idea,' said Sylvia, from the kitchen.

'Thanks, Gran. We're going to have to join a load of Facebook groups. Our notifications are going to go mad.' She let out a sigh. 'Still, if it helps find out what happened to Owen, it'll be worth it, and we can always politely leave the Facebook groups after that.'

'So, we're looking for groups for dog walkers, runners, and anglers.'

'Don't forget shift workers,' said Sylvia. 'Like nurses, doctors, postman and delivery drivers.'

Zoe was Googling. 'There's a Wootton Night Owls group.' She read the description. *'For anyone who works shifts or suffers from insomnia. If you're awake or at work when other people are the opposite, and you're looking for a bit of company and humour, this group is for you.'*

'Sounds like your mother should join,' Sylvia joked.

'Actually – that's given me an idea. Can we use your Facebook account to post from, Gran? It'll look less suss coming from an oldie.'

Finn nudged her.

'You wait 'til you get to your sixties, young lady. See how you like being called old.'

'Just joking. D'you want to log into your Facebook account and chuck your phone over?'

Sylvia washed her hands and picked up her phone. She clicked on the Facebook icon, muttering to herself about how much she hated technology and social media. 'Damn. I got as far as logging in and now the app's got to update.' She passed it to Zoe and went back to her shortbread.

Zoe waited. 'Right. Updated. Logged in. Aww. Your profile pic is of you and Grandad in Italy.'

Sylvia gulped. It was why she'd stopped using Facebook. The reminders of Ron and their life together. The anniversaries. His illness. Such bittersweet memories.

'Here we are. Wootton Night Owls,' said Zoe. 'I'll request to join as you. You never know. Mum and I saw the balloon. Other people must have seen it too. We can't be the only people who were awake then.'

Sylvia dolloped the mixture onto a board, rolled it flat, then used the metal cutter to form shortbread squares. She very carefully placed these on greaseproof paper on a baking tray.

Finn piped up. 'So far, I've posted in Wootton Anglers, the Wootton Morning Run and on the Wootton Royal Mail Delivery Office page. We should get a few replies from those.'

'Well done,' said Sylvia.

'Wootton Night Owls has just approved Gran's join request. I'll post in there now.' Zoe spoke aloud as she was typing. 'Thanks for letting me join. Slightly strange request: was anyone awake between 6.30am and 7.15am ...' She finished it in silence.

'I think doctors and nurses tend to finish their shifts around 8am so they'll probably be a bit later, Sylvia added.'

'Have you set the alarm for the oven?' Zoe asked Finn.

'Sure have. I might eat them all though, while you're out.'

'I'm interested to see what comes from these Facebook groups. If we get any interesting replies,' Sylvia said to Finn, 'will you text us?'

'Will do. I'll have a read of the comments on the local paper's Facebook page too.'

'Changing the subject for a mo...' Zoe slid off her seat and shuffled over to Sylvia. 'Has Dad talked to you about this promotion he's been offered?'

Sylvia shook her head. 'You could broach the subject with him. He's your dad. You're entitled to ask about his plans too.'

'Thanks, Gran. I might.' She pulled one of her plaits round and inspected her hair for split ends. 'I don't want to stress Mum out asking her about it. Do you think he's going to give up on her and move away?'

Chapter 16

'There's Trudy,' Zoe told Sylvia, pointing at a young woman who was behind the bar of the Windmill Inn, taking glasses out of the dishwasher and polishing them. Zoe knew Trudy from when she'd worked at the pub.

It was strange, being in the bar before it opened. Quieter, calmer and more spacious. Sylvia was looking forward to hearing what the barmaid could tell them about Owen.

Two other staff members were on duty, another woman who was refilling the mixer shelves from plastic crates. She was wearing baggy denim shorts with thick black tights underneath. A tall man was sweeping out one of the fires. He had kindling and firelighters in a box, and a lurcher lay like a lion statue on the rug. It was the chap they'd seen on the search yesterday.

Zoe introduced her grandmother to Trudy.

'Anna has asked us to help find her husband,' Sylvia told Trudy. 'We're private investigators. We've come to ask a few questions.'

'The boss is in the cellar.'

'Great, thanks. We'll speak to him in a minute. Alright to have a quick chat with you first?'

'Sure,' Trudy replied, glancing around nervously. 'Shall we go and sit over in that booth? It's a bit more private.' She led them over and they sat down. 'What would you like to know?'

'How long have you worked here?'

'Two years. Just before Zoe started.' She smiled at Zoe, who was a similar age to her. 'Lara and I started at the same time. She's the one doing the mixer bottles and crisps.'

'And who's this?' Sylvia pointed to the guy making the fire.

'That's Todd. He, George, Lara and I are the full-time staff who work behind the bar. There are about ten part-timers. George is the head barman. Owen and Phil are the chefs.'

'How do you get on with Owen?'

She smiled. 'We all get on well with him. He's a really nice guy. Great chef, good boss. Is there any news?'

'I don't think so. Not yet. How was he in the period up to him going missing? Did he seem happy? Was anything bothering him?'

'Lara and I talked about this. He is generally a happy bloke, but we've all noticed that something has been bothering him for a couple of months.' She fiddled with the salt and pepper pots on the table. 'He's always laid back, but he's been snappy and short-tempered recently.'

'When did you start noticing this?'

'When his brother took over as manager.'

'Was that two months ago?'

'Roughly. The beginning of September.'

'And what happened?' Sylvia was watching Trudy's face. Her cheeks were flushed, and a rash was creeping up her neck.

'They started arguing.'

'What about? Can you give examples?'

'Owen would say how we do things and John would say, "Oh, we're not going to do it like that anymore". Owen would explain why we did things that way and would ask why we needed to change them, given that the current systems already worked. But John wasn't interested. He wanted Owen to say, "Yes, that's fine, no problem"– and a lot of the time he did, but when he believed an important principle was at stake, he would put his foot down.'

'Can you give us an example?' asked Sylvia.

'Yeah. John wants us to use frozen food because it's cheaper and Owen says it doesn't taste the same or have the same nutritional value.'

Sylvia was thinking about the frozen fruit that recipes use sometimes. 'What else?'

'John wants to get rid of some of the staff. Make us do more and work harder so that he can increase his profits.'

That didn't sound good.

'Owen doesn't believe in that. He says people need to feel valued to get the best out of them. He manages the catering staff.'

The two brothers clearly had very different management styles.

'How does that work?' Sylvia was wondering about George.

'Extremely well. In all the time I've worked here, not one of the staff has left because they were unhappy with the management.' She paused and glanced at Sylvia. 'Now everyone wants to leave.'

It was definitely a good move, talking to Trudy. Sylvia now had several more questions on her list of things to ask John.

'Oh dear. That sounds difficult. How do George and Owen get on?'

Trudy frowned. 'OK, that's one person who didn't get on with Owen. He wanted to work in the kitchen and Owen wouldn't have it.'

'Because?'

'Owen liked everything done properly. He was all for talent and passion, but he said George needed to undertake training.' Trudy fanned her cheeks.

Sylvia nodded. It sounded fair enough. 'What are you going to do?'

She threw her hands open. 'We're all hoping Owen's coming back. He is, right? He's got to.' Her eyebrows were raised and her eyes wide.

'We all hope so. Were the arguments between John and Owen all about the pub?'

'Pretty much.'

'Does Gail get involved with the place much?'

'Sometimes. I think the plan is for her to take over managing staff while John manages the business.'

'What about Anna?' Zoe chipped in. 'Does she come in?'

'Oh, yes. You know what this place is like. It's the social hub of the village. Anna comes in with friends. She pops in for coffee. She comes in for lunch sometimes. All very cordial.' Her face clouded over when she finished speaking.

'But?'

'She *did*. She doesn't anymore. I don't know why not. She suddenly stopped coming in.'

'How strange. When was this?'

'Two months ago. Something like that.'

'Did it coincide with John and Gail taking the pub over?'

'It might have done.'

Sylvia and Zoe glanced at each other, and Sylvia made a mental note to ask Anna about this. And John.

'Do you know what Owen's professional plans are?'

'Not in detail, but when the previous owners said they were selling, he was interested – until John said he wanted to buy a share. Owen didn't want to go into partnership.' A wistful expression stole over her youthful features.

Sylvia wondered if Trudy knew Owen was looking for another pub. 'What makes you think that?'

'He suddenly stopped talking about plans for this place and started having meetings – at weird times of the day sometimes too.' She examined her hands and turned them over to check her fingernails. 'And he's been asking about some of the local pubs.'

It sounded like something had happened.

'You mean, with a view to buying one of them instead?'

Trudy nodded. 'Think so.'

'Was there a dispute with his brother, do you know?'

'We aren't sure. But a couple of weeks ago, Owen was extremely upset. He went storming upstairs to talk to John and they had a huge row. We could all hear it down here. I've never seen Owen so angry.'

'I know it might feel a bit awkward, but can you remember what you heard them saying?'

'Yeah. The ceilings here are paper thin.' She blushed. 'Owen said, "You had to, didn't you? Just like when we were kids. Whenever I had something you wanted, you always took it away from me".'

Sylvia was nodding. She had wondered about something like this.

Sibling rivalry.

'He also said, "Just for once, why couldn't we have shared?"'

'Did it sound serious? Lots of siblings have those sorts of rows.'

'It's hard to gauge. We thought so.'

'Any idea what gave you that impression?'

She frowned as she reflected. 'Because Owen never gets riled. That he did on this occasion, we knew it was about something important to him.'

'What were John's replies?'

'He kept saying Owen didn't understand business. That he was a dreamer.'

'Can't have been easy things for any of you to overhear.'

Tears welled up in Trudy's eyes. 'Where is he? Has something happened to him?'

'Why do you ask that?'

'We're all wondering the same thing. Because he'd never leave this place. He loved it. And he adored Anna.'

Chapter 17

'Wow,' Zoe whispered to Sylvia. They'd said good-bye to Trudy at the pub and were on their way to speak to John.

Todd had finished making the fires. Both were roaring away and the lurcher had stretched out on the rug by the hearth.

'Something has *definitely* happened here,' Sylvia replied, mirroring Zoe's hushed tones. 'I can feel it. I don't mean murder. I mean something to do with the pub.'

'It's odd that Anna said Owen wanted to buy a share and Gail said he didn't.'

'Exactly.'

'I've got Trudy's new phone number now if we need to follow anything up.'

John was in the basement when they arrived to speak to him.

'Alright?' He was wearing a white, double-breasted chef's jacket, checked blue and white trousers and a cloth 'zandana' on his head. He was doing something with pipes and frothy solution in a plastic container. 'You two came to the search, didn't you?' He checked his watch. 'I'll be leading another one after lunch, combing the shoreline this time between Wootton and Kingsdown.'

'That's right. I'm Sylvia Blix. This is my granddaughter, Zoe.'

'Blix? You related to the DI bloke?'

'He's my dad,' Zoe said proudly. 'You taken up cooking?' She gestured to his clothes.

'Had to. Can't get a temporary chef for love nor money, and Phil can't do it all. George is helping out a bit but when it's busy, I need him behind the bar.'

'We'll be sampling your food later. We've booked a table for lunch.' Sylvia collected her thoughts. 'We're here now though on a slightly different basis. Albeit with the same aim in mind.'

He frowned. 'And what would that be?'

'We do private investigations for friends in the village. Anna's asked us to look into your brother's disappearance.'

'Has she? Well, I'm pleased to hear someone is. The police don't seem to be doing much.' John's tone was gruff and he kicked a beer barrel. 'When someone's low risk, they seem to assume they'll turn up on their own.'

Sylvia could see his frustration.

'But you're not going to turn up if you're face down in a ditch. Are you?' He paused. 'Or washed up on the beach?'

'Is that what you think has happened to him?'

He shrugged. 'I've no idea. But I'm worried sick and it's hard not to think about the worst-case scenario. I keep ringing the police. So does Anna. But they won't tell us anything. I'm waiting for your son to call me back.'

Sylvia understood perfectly why Anna and John were worried.

He chucked a pipe on the ground. 'All I know is, Owen pulled out of the balloon ride at the last minute, and no-one's seen or heard from him since.'

'Did your brother call you or text you to say he wasn't coming on the balloon ride?'

'You've already asked me this. He rang from the car.'

'It's just your wife told us he texted.'

He shrugged. 'She's probably got confused or forgotten. It's been a very stressful time for all of us. We're exhausted.'

'Fair enough. How did he sound on the phone?'

'Like he normally does. But it was shortly after 5am, my wife was flapping about whether she was wearing enough layers, and I was loading gear into the Land Rover.'

'When he said he was going to go to McDonald's and then home to bed, did you believe him?'

His forehead crunched into a frown. 'Of course. Why wouldn't I? It wasn't out of character for him at all. He's been behaving weirdly for a couple of months now.'

Ah. Good. She could ask about the pub. 'What sort of weird?'

'Whispered phone calls. Dashing out for secret business meetings without any notice. Before and after the pub closed.'

'I suppose that's the long hours, is it?'

He nodded. 'He didn't think I'd noticed, but I had. The pub game is a small world. That's why when he cancelled the balloon ride, I assumed that was where he'd gone.'

'Meetings with who?' She was wondering if John knew about The Rattling Cat.

'No idea. He didn't tell me.'

'You mean like a rival pub, or something?'

John's eyes narrowed. 'I've heard all sorts. I wanted to go into partnership with him but Owen wasn't interested. He wanted to do his own thing.'

'But would he have had a meeting at 6am?'

He snorted. 'You obviously don't know the pub business. We work long and anti-social hours. It's not easy to arrange meetings. We have to grab them when people are free. I met an asparagus farmer at 6am the other week. He was on his way to the market and it was the only time we could both make.' He blew into the pipe. 'If my brother was meeting someone, perhaps they happened to be around at that time. Walking the dog or going for a run? And Owen decided to go for it.'

'Any idea why McDonald's? Is he a fan? I wouldn't have thought it would be the first choice of many chefs.'

'Your guess is as good as mine. It's one of few places open at that time, unless you go into Dover. Easy to get to. Plus, less likely to be seen, if he was worried about that.' He shrugged. 'Alternatively, it's possible they didn't have had any food in at home that he fancied. Like meat. My brother likes a good fry-up and Anna's into all that vegan stuff.'

'Had Owen been looking forward to the hot air balloon ride? When it was first suggested, was he keen?'

'Oh, yes. We all were. Owen wanted to learn to fly.'

'What I'm finding difficult to understand is why he had a change of heart so late in the day.'

'Can't answer for him, I'm afraid. But – like I say, it wasn't out of character.'

'If he was tired and hungry, why get up at all? Why not sleep in and have breakfast at home?'

'It's possible that the "tired and hungry" thing was a ruse. If he was waiting for a meeting to be confirmed, which he didn't want us to know about, or one came up at short notice, it's the perfect cover.'

'I suppose.'

'My brother is determined when he puts his mind to something. And more than a bit sneaky.'

'What *had* he put his mind to?'

'Buying a pub. And I was pleased for him. I've been encouraging him to step out of the sweat of the kitchen for years.'

'Let's come onto that now. Your wife says you've bought the pub. I thought you were managing it?'

'That's right. We were, until a couple of weeks ago.' He said it matter-of-fact-ly, as though they'd bought a new car, not a business.

'Before you bought the place, did you know your brother wanted to buy a share?'

'I don't know where you've got that from. That's what *we* wanted but he wasn't interested.'

'Did you discuss with him why not?'

'Of course. He just said he wanted to do his own thing.'

'Why would Anna say the opposite?'

He shrugged. 'I don't think he always tells her the truth. Listen. I love my brother, but our relationship hasn't always been easy. We're chalk and cheese. He has lots of hare-brained ideas and they change by the day. It's difficult to keep up.' He raised his eyebrows. 'I've learned not to take any of them seriously, I'm afraid.'

Zoe spluttered.

'The pub staff mentioned the argument you and your brother had. What was that about?'

'That was my fault. I had to give the sellers our offer and Owen said he wasn't interested. I was gutted and I'm afraid I rather lost my temper with him.' He cast his gaze down. 'I was hoping that at last we could do something together.'

This was the opposite of what Trudy had told them.

'Mr Field, can we rewind a moment, please?' Sylvia asked.

He frowned.

'Anna told us Owen wanted to buy a share of the pub and you're saying he did not. You can't both be correct. Did your brother have a change of heart?'

'Not that I know of. He told us from the start he didn't want to go into business with us.'

'Why is Anna saying he did?'

He shook his head. 'I don't know. You'll have to ask her. It's possible she got the wrong end of the stick. I think she's a bit yoga-y about business...'

'What does that mean?'

'Vague.' He changed tone. 'But – the argument was over in a flash. I calmed down and Owen started looking for other venues. He was more excited than I've seen him in ages. It really wasn't a big deal.'

Sylvia was trying to think how to phrase her next question. 'The staff say the atmosphere's been tense for much longer than that. Is that true?' She was thinking about what Trudy had heard Owen say to his brother.

Whenever I had something you wanted, you always took it away from me.

John stopped what he was doing and seemed to study the pipe he was cleaning. 'He's my little brother, Mrs Blix. However difficult our relationship is sometimes, I look out for him.'

'It's a habit I got into when I was a social worker,' Sylvia told him, trying to look apologetic. 'Always wondering about sibling rivalry.'

'Is there a question here?'

'I suppose what I'm struggling with is that the staff say Owen rarely gets riled. That it was a shock when he found out you'd bought the pub and it made him really angry. That's quite different from what you're saying. Isn't it?'

He tried to conceal a tut. 'Yes. It is. We had a row. Like all brothers do from time to time. I was annoyed with him but I got over it quickly. As I *also* said.' He sighed.

'Do you get on with Anna? Like her?'

'She's perfectly lovely. Just very vegan-yoga.'

Sylvia cringed at his expression. 'OK. Thank you. All the staff talk about Owen in very complimentary terms. They say how nice he is to work with. How much he cares about staff welfare. How popular he is with the customers.'

He nodded. 'All true. Everyone loves him.'

Zoe was watching carefully.

'Yet he's disappeared.'

John narrowed his eyes, nodding slowly while he thought about what to say. 'I'm not getting your drift. Do only unpleasant people disappear?'

'I'm just wondering if anyone might have had a reason to harm him.'

'We'll find him. I have no doubt about that.'

It was a strange answer.

'Your wife said that your barman, George, picked you up when you landed the balloon on Saturday morning.'

'That's correct. He's a friend of mine. It was a private flight, just my wife and me. We're both experienced balloonists so there was no need for a large crew. The main thing is having someone to meet you with a car to pick you up and take you back to your own vehicle. George lives near where we inflated the balloon and took off. He helped us set up, followed the balloon and met us.'

'Does he normally crew for you?'

'No. This was a special occasion because it was our wedding anniversary. He said he'd help out.'

'Why didn't you ask your usual people?'

'I did. Everyone was busy.'

'I see. Turning to Owen and Anna now – how do they get on?'

'As far as I know, they're extremely happy. Always have been. Owen adores her.'

'No affairs?'

'Good Lord, no. If two people are a match made in heaven, it's Anna and my brother.'

Sylvia smiled. 'He doesn't mind the 'vegan-yoga' thing?'

'Apparently not.'

Sylvia couldn't help thinking about John's McDonald's comment. If Owen ate meat away from home, might he also have been having an affair?

John checked his watch. 'Look, I'm going to have to fly. We've got lunch starting at midday and I need to help with prep.' He stared at her and Zoe. 'Then we're doing a search along the shoreline at 3.30pm. Are you coming to help?'

Chapter 18

W arm, woody air hit Ellie as she entered the bar of the Windmill Inn to meet the family for lunch. Pop hits tinkled away. Zoe had texted her to say they were sitting in an alcove to the right of the fire.

The place was heaving. Not one empty table in sight, and two-deep at the bar from one end to the other. People were ordering food and drinks, hanging up coats and scarves, collecting crisps, cutlery and condiments. The smells wafting around were making her mouth water.

Ellie felt a stab of sadness that Owen wasn't in the kitchen, cooking his mouth-watering roasts. She remembered how, once all the meals were cooked, he'd often sit at the end of the bar, chef's jacket unbuttoned, having a drink. Customers liked seeing the man whose hands and expertise had prepared their meal, and they'd often chat to him and offer him a drink.

She joined her group, sinking onto the empty seat next to Sylvia and opposite Zoe and Finn.

'You just missed John,' Zoe told her mum. 'He came out of the kitchen to grab a couple of lemons from behind the bar. He's cooking temporarily and George is helping him.'

'I can't help noticing that *one* person has got what they wanted as a result of Owen going missing then.' Sylvia raised her eyebrows suggestively.

'That's true, sadly, isn't it?' replied Ellie.

Zoe – who was always hungry – had her food face on. 'Right. They've got roasts with all the trimmings. Pork, beef, chicken, lamb. On the specials board they've got several new game dishes, rabbit and venison sausages, and pan-fried sea bass.'

Ellie remembered the board she'd seen outside the pub the day before. 'I don't remember Owen doing this much game.'

'Apparently, they've got a new supplier. From John's old pub.'

Throughout their meal, Finn's phone was beeping continuously with notifications. 'Bingo,' he said. 'We've got someone else who saw the balloon just after it took off.'

'That's fantastic,' said Ellie. 'What do they say?'

'He was out running with his dog. Only saw the balloon for a short period of time and saw *three* people in the basket.'

'That's a result,' said Ellie.

'What do you want me to say?' he asked Ellie.

'Nothing for the moment, but can you screenshot his profile? Given a man's gone missing on his way to the hot air balloon ride, I would prefer to ask this runner face to face what he saw. We're probably going to need him as a witness.'

In the absence of Owen, it seemed to be all hands on deck at the Windmill Inn. Gail and Trudy were helping in the kitchen with the Sunday lunch rush, bringing out steaming plates of food from the kitchen and collecting up empty dishes.

At that moment, the main door opened and Dave appeared.

'Hey up,' said Zoe. 'Dad incoming.'

He was wearing a suit and tie, his expression serious.

'Think it's safe to assume he's not going to be joining us for lunch,' said Ellie.

He headed straight for the end of the bar, spoke briefly to a barmaid and then disappeared into the kitchen.

Chapter 19

The windows in the pub kitchen were steamed up when Ellie went in after lunch to find George. The radio was on loud, playing the local news. He and John had finished serving meals and were clearing up. There didn't seem to be any sign of the other chef John had mentioned.

John had taken off his chef's jacket and zandana, and was in a white T-shirt. He was unloading a steaming dishwasher and stacking plates on the shelves above the worktops. By the back door, several rabbits and pheasants hung from hooks.

Ellie noticed a cluster of scabs in John's hair. 'What's happened to your head?'

'Oh, it's nothing serious. I bashed my head downstairs in the cellar the other night. Wasn't looking what I was doing and walked backwards into a beam.'

George was wiping down the stainless-steel worktops. Like John, he was wearing checked trousers and a white jacket which was fully open, with a fluorescent orange running vest underneath.

Ellie recognised him from Finn's gig at the Rattling Cat. 'OK to have a quick chat, George?'

George looked at John for permission.

'Sure,' he said.

George grabbed a can of Coke from the fridge and followed Ellie out into the private part of the pub garden where they could talk.

'Yeah, I crewed for John and Gail on Saturday morning.' The can fizzed as he opened it. He took several gulps. 'They only did a short trip and I often go out for a run at that time, so it was no trouble. I'm training for the Dover half-marathon.'

'Talk me through what happened.'

'I met them at the car park on the beach side of Hawking Down. Helped them get the balloon ready to fly. Stayed by the basket until it took off and followed them until they went behind the trees. When they were landing, John called me and said where to meet them with the Land Rover. You never quite know but you can make an informed guess from the wind direction.'

'And who went up in the balloon basket?'

'John and Gail. It was their anniversary.'

'Did you see Owen?'

He shook his head. 'When I arrived, John told me Owen had decided not to come.'

'Were John and Gail worried about Owen?'

They'd asked Anna and Gail the same question, but she was interested to find out what George would say.

He shook his head. 'Not that I picked up on. I got the impression they weren't surprised he'd cancelled.'

'What gave you that idea?'

'I said something like, "No Owen?" and John said it wasn't the first time he'd ducked out of things at the last minute. He seemed quite upset, actually.'

'My daughter's boyfriend was telling us about your nickname at school.' She softened her tone.

'Oh, Finn.' He chuckled.

'You're still into cooking, I see?'

His face lit up. 'I love it.'

'Do you help Owen in the kitchen?' She knew the answer of course but wanted to check how George felt.

He shook his head. 'Nope. I offered loads of times, but he didn't want me near the kitchen. Was really possessive about the place.'

Ellie nodded.

'Shame really,' George added. 'I had some good ideas for the menus.'

'Are you angry with him about that?'

He gave an irritated shrug. 'Yeah. Course. He looked down on me. It was out of order.'

'You didn't wish him harm or anything like that?'

He frowned, clocking the suggestion. 'Absolutely not.'

'Whose idea was it to put more game on the menu?'

'John's and Todd's. Owen wasn't keen on it but it's really popular with the customers. John's brought his supplier over from the pub in Canterbury.'

She caught the sadness in his voice. And – was there a trace of something else?

He drained the Coke and crunched the can in his hand. 'In the hospitality industry, we all want to get ahead, you know?'

'But you're working in the kitchen now, I gather.' She watched for his reaction.

He beamed at her. 'Yes. I'm the new head chef.' Then seemed to think better of what he'd said. 'Until Owen comes back, of course.'

Chapter 20

It was Trudy's night off when Ellie and Zoe next went back into the pub to speak to her.

'I'll text her,' said Zoe. 'See if we can pop round to her flat. I know where she lives.'

Ellie had Rebus on the lead and Zoe had Agatha – who Dave hadn't collected – on hers. Neither dog could be trusted not to run round tables, begging, or dart behind the bar sniffing out the crisp boxes and pork scratchings.

'Let's drop these two back at the windmill,' said Ellie.

Zoe's phone dinged. 'Trudy says that's fine. She's going out at 7pm but is home now. It's flat B on the ground floor.'

Trudy's flat was in a large brick and flint house in one of the roads off the high street. The building was surrounded by a tall wooden fence. They entered through the gate and were soon at the front door.

Trudy buzzed them in and met them at the flat door. She was in a red corduroy skirt and cream jersey top, her pink hair tied up in high bunches. One eye had make-up on. She held up a mascara tube. 'Hot date,' she said. 'Come in.'

Ellie smiled and they followed her into a high-ceilinged hall. Fairy lights twinkled over a large, gold, Gothic mirror. A tabby cat came lolloping towards them.

'That's Mackerel,' said Trudy. 'Would you like a drink of anything?'

'Don't worry,' Zoe told her. 'We can see you're busy.'

In the lounge, an open fire was roaring away. On the floor, on a sheepskin rug, a young woman sat cross-legged, adding logs to the basket and prodding the embers with a poker. Beside her were knitting needles and a ball of pink wool.

'Have a seat. This is my sister, Hilary.'

They said hello.

'Quick question, if that's OK.' Ellie spoke in a low tone. 'Who supplies game to the pub?'

'Todd.' Trudy began applying mascara.

Mackerel sauntered over to Hilary and started poking the wool with a pudgy paw.

Ellie smiled. 'A lot of it?'

'Yep. Owen would never buy from him, but when John and Gail took over as managers, that changed and Todd started working behind the bar. He and John go back years. They had a business together once.'

'Why didn't Owen want to buy from Todd?'

'Owen's fastidious about provenance, so that customers know what they're eating and where it's come from. But also so animals are only caught and shot when they're allowed to be, not when they've got babies. I'm not saying Todd does the latter, but Owen was never sure.'

Given Trudy and Zoe had heard similar rumours, there had to be some truth to them. It was important to check though.

'Can I ask how you know this?' Ellie asked.

'I heard Todd offer Owen some poached game a few months ago. One of the barmaids had dropped a bowl of soup behind the bar and I was getting the mop and filling the bucket to clean it up before one of us had an accident. I heard the whole conversation.'

'What did Owen say?'

'Unless Todd could confirm where the meat came from, the answer was no.'

'How did Todd react to that?'

'He did all the wink-wink thing and called Owen "mate". Tried saying it didn't really matter, but Owen wasn't having it.'

'Good for him.'

Trudy put her mascara down. 'The thing is, you were in the pub earlier. A lot of the customers eating game don't mind about sourcing or seasons. The townies and city-dwellers. But those of us who've grown up in villages do.'

Ellie agreed. 'It's rural life, isn't it?'

'Word has already got round about all the game on the menu now,' said Trudy. 'People are going to ask questions about where he's getting it from.'

This was true. Ellie had noticed it on the board outside the pub.

'And you know what Nick and Charlie Matthews are like about meat sources. They make Owen look relaxed. Nick's already been in to speak to John.'

That was interesting.

From the floor, Hilary pitched in. 'He's going to lose customers. The locals will all go up the road to the Rattling Cat.'

And, by the sound of it, between them, John, George and Todd weren't now giving the village a choice.

Chapter 21
MONDAY

The next morning, after getting up to let Rebus out and check the Blix Blitz job rota – as was her usual routine – Ellie took a cup of tea upstairs for Sylvia and herself. The two of them were in their nighties, sitting in Ellie's bed, chatting, duvet over their legs, sheet masks over their faces.

'I'm scared to move in case this thing falls off,' said Sylvia through lips that barely moved. 'What did Zoe say it does? Hydration and what?'

'Radiance.'

They caught each other's eye.

'We must look a right pair of numpties.' Sylvia chuckled.

Rebus was on the bed between them, snoring.

'I've just checked my email,' said Ellie. 'The new washing machine and tumble dryer are being delivered after nine this morning.'

'Thank goodness,' Sylvia replied. 'I know it's a pain buying new ones, but Sarge and Sean can't do all the laundry with two washing machines and one dryer.' She patted her mask.

'I agree.'

'Do you want to talk about Dave? Are you going to speak to him about this move and promotion?'

'I sent him a text last night asking if we could discuss it. I understand him considering it. Things have changed for both of us, and it's made me re-evaluate my life and whether *I* want to stay in Wootton. I don't blame him for doing the same.'

Sylvia smiled kindly. 'Excuse me. You better not go anywhere,' she joked. 'You've got me living here now. And Mum's only up the road.'

'The thing is, because Dave and I got together so young, we've both had to find out what life is like without the other.' Ellie was thinking aloud. 'That opens up questions; pushes doors open. It was inevitable something like this would happen.'

'That's all very philosophical. How do you *feel* about it though?'

For Ellie, it was as though a hand was creeping round her heart, another round her throat. The same as happened whenever she thought about Dave and what she wanted.

'Honestly? Still conflicted. And fed up with it.' The tightening around her organs scared her. 'It's why I understand him considering moving away.'

Sylvia nodded. 'I can relate totally. When Ron died, I went through a similar process. I even contemplated going to Australia at one point.'

'Wow. I never considered going that far.' Ellie patted the mask around her mouth. 'Were you serious?'

'About wanting a change, yes. That was probably partly why I invited myself to stay here with you and Zoe.'

Ellie chuckled. Sylvia's "it's-cold-at-my-house" ruse hadn't fooled Ellie one bit, especially since the boiler had been on the blink at the windmill at the time. But she'd been extremely grateful for Sylvia's help and company back then – and ever since. 'I doubt we can compete with Australia but we're very glad you chose us.'

'*Mum?*' came Zoe's voice from downstairs. The alarm in it was unmistakeable. 'Gran? A body's been found.'

'Oh, no,' said Ellie. She threw back the covers, yanked the sheet off her face and leapt out of bed.

'Coming,' Sylvia yelled back. She peeled her mask off and followed Ellie out of the bedroom.

The two of them clattered down the stairs, Rebus leading the way.

The news was on the TV.

'The circumstances of the death are being treated as suspicious,' said the presenter. She was standing on the beach, wrapped in a red scarf and long, black coat. *'The identity of the man is known to the police but has not been shared yet. I'll turn now to Detective Inspector Dave Blix of Kent Police.'*

'Yes, good morning,' said Dave. He was on the stones, Deal pier behind him. There was a white crime scene tent to his left.

'We were called at 7.13pm last night by a member of the public who had been fishing when he saw the body of a man wash up on the beach.'

'A male, then,' whispered Ellie.

'The deceased is in his forties,' Dave continued. *'We are in the process of informing his family and are not releasing his name yet.'*

'That's Owen's age,' Zoe whispered back.

Sylvia poked her. 'Ssh, both of you.'

'Sadly, we are treating it as a suspicious death. Enquiries have commenced to establish the full circumstances of this tragic incident.'

A phone number appeared on the screen below Dave.

'Did you see or hear anything?' he asked the viewers. *'Were you in the area of Deal pier at the time? If you have information that could help us understand the circumstances of his death, please let us know on the number below.'*

The camera panned out to show the shoreline and the whole of Deal pier.

'I wonder if it's Owen.' Zoe voiced the concern of them all.

'Everyone's going to be asking the same question. I'm sure they'll release the name as soon as they can.'

'I know. Poor Anna and John though. They're going to be worried sick.'

Chapter 22

'Have you seen the news?' Anna gabbled down the phone at Ellie.

Ellie switched it onto loudspeaker so Sylvia and Zoe could hear.

'Yes,' replied Ellie, her voice tight with anticipation.

'I've rung the police and asked if it's Owen, but they can't say at the moment.'

Ellie heard the anguish in Anna's snatched breaths. The waiting was going to be unbearable for her and John.

Sylvia put one arm round Ellie, the other round Zoe.

Ellie's head was spinning. It must be awful for Anna, not knowing where her husband was. She would have been hoping for good news, and was probably now scared out of her wits that the body was Owen's. 'Did the police say anything else?'

'Something about it possibly changing the missing person case, and that they have lines of enquiry they need to pursue.'

'Oh?'

'That's what I thought. I asked what that means but they weren't able to explain further.'

'You still want us to carry on investigating though, do you?'

'Oh, yes, please. Definitely.' She paused. 'There's one other thing ...'

'What's that?'

'Jaq's got to go home, and I don't want to be on my own. Could I possibly sleep on your couch for a couple of days?'

'Of course you can. We'd love to have you. Grab some stuff and come on over. If we aren't here, there's a key in the outhouse under the cat's bed by the door.'

'She can have my room,' Zoe whispered to her mum. 'I'll have the couch or stay at Finn's.'

'We'll see you shortly,' Ellie said, and rang off.

Zoe showed Ellie her phone screen. On it was an enlarged screenshot of the pier behind Dave's head, from the news bulletin. Someone had placed a gnome in between the railings of the old pier.

It was the same gnome that had been outside the windmill on Saturday morning.

Ellie slapped her forehead. 'Darn. I forgot to say – the Field's doorbell thingy is connected to an app on Gail's phone. Zo, could you arrange with her to have a look at it? See if we can identify the person who's doing this nonsense? It's not funny and it needs to stop.'

'No probs,' said Zoe.

Sylvia was straight on the phone to the vicar. 'Well, unless there are two identical gnomes, the one on the pier is definitely the one that was outside the windmill. And there was a different one outside Anna and Owen's house.'

The vicar's perplexed tones reverberated down the line.

'I'll WhatsApp you the image so you can check if it's the one from Mr Blackman's grave.'

More questions from the vicar.

'No, we've no idea how it got here … or onto the pier. Hopefully they'll have CCTV there.' She told him about the app on Gail's phone.

Ellie let Sylvia finish her conversation. She filled the kettle and switched it on to boil. Dropped a couple of slices of bread into the toaster and pushed the lever down.

CLICK.

The lights went off. The kettle; fridge; toaster.

Ellie let out a loud groan. 'Not again. I thought what's-his-name had fixed it.'

'Brian,' said Zoe.

'Got to go,' Sylvia told the vicar.

Zoe got her phone out. 'I'll call him. He's going to install a new consumer unit this week and change some of the wiring outside. He hoped the temporary measures would get us through 'til then.'

Sylvia scuttled towards the back door. 'Quick. We need to switch off all the appliances in the outhouse and unplug them.'

Ellie and Finn followed her.

'Keep the dog in the house,' Ellie shouted over her shoulder.

'I'll grab a couple of torches,' said Zoe.

As expected, the outhouse was in darkness. Sylvia opened the door and charged in. 'Argh, there's water everywhere.' On the concrete floor, water was seeping through her sheepskin slippers.

'A machine must've flooded.' Finn ran over to one and began unplugging them all.

Ellie waded through the water and started opening the windows that ran the length of the building. 'There's so much water, we won't know which until we can see underneath,' said Ellie.

'I'll get the mop and a load of dog towels,' said Sylvia. 'Change these slippers for my wellies.'

Zoe arrived with two torches. 'Oh, crikey. Dad's CDs are in here too. I've left a message for Brian. He's not answering his phone at the moment.'

'I think he goes to the gym first thing in the morning,' said Finn. 'I'll nip over and have a quick word with him. See if he can come here when he's finished.'

'Thank you,' said Ellie.

'If we unplug everything in here, will the power come back on in the windmill?' asked Zoe.

'Not until we've got all the water away from the sockets,' Ellie replied, grabbing up piles of dry sheets from on top of the machines. 'Quite apart from us now being without heating, if I don't get the laundry done, I'm going to lose customers.'

Ellie turned round and saw Anna. Hair in a scruffy ponytail, a small rucksack over her shoulder, her face the picture of misery.

Rebus was at her side. On seeing the water, he leaped into it and began pawing at a ball which was floating.

'Oh dear,' said Anna. 'I couldn't have picked a worse time, could I?'

Chapter 23

Two hours later, semi-calm had returned to the windmill. The Blixes had mopped up all the water in the outhouse, and got the power back on in the main building.

Anna was upstairs in Zoe's bedroom.

Ellie and Sylvia were on the landing, outside the door.

'I think it's beginning to hit her,' whispered Ellie. 'I know she's said from the start that something's happened to Owen, but I suspect a lot of that was about protecting herself from the worst, if it turned out to be the case.'

'I agree,' Sylvia whispered back. 'I would imagine it's sinking in that something has probably happened.'

Ellie knocked gently. 'Is it alright to come in?'

'Just a minute,' came Anna's reply.

They heard nose-blowing.

'OK. Come in.'

Ellie pushed open the door and they filed in.

Anna looked tiny on the left-hand side of Zoe's king-size bed, curled up in a ball. On the bedside cabinet, a photograph of Finn smiled at them from a silver frame.

'Don't lose hope,' Ellie said, sitting down on the bed. 'I think the police would have told you by now if the body was Owen's.'

'Do you really?'

Ellie studied her friend's face. Anna looked desperate. The awful anguish in her eyes; her deeper-than-usual eye sockets; her clenched jaw.

'I agree. In some ways it's good news the police haven't been back in touch,' Sylvia said gently.

Ellie put her hand on Anna's arm. 'I would try to keep thinking positively, if you can.' She checked Anna's mug which was untouched, a couple of digestive biscuits next to it. 'Would you like a fresh cup of tea?'

'Thanks, but I can't keep anything down at the moment. And I'm scared to sleep. I keep having horrible dreams. Imagining Owen in the marsh or lying at the bottom of a cliff – or, now, washed up on the beach...'

'Oh, sweetie.' Ellie gave her a hug. 'That's very hard.'

'We need to broach something a bit sensitive,' Sylvia said softly.

'What?' asked Anna, dabbing at her face with a tissue.

'Well, something we haven't touched on yet – and perhaps now should – is whether anybody might have had a reason to harm Owen.'

Anna stared at her in disbelief.

Ellie was interested to hear how Anna was going to answer, particularly with John buying the pub, George wanting to get into the kitchen, and Owen having business meetings.

Anna frowned, as if she was finding it hard to contemplate the question. 'No. *No-one.* This is the thing. Everyone loves him. He's a really genuine, decent guy. Kind, honest, caring.'

'We know the staff have a high opinion of him. Did he have any disagreements with anyone?'

'Only his brother.'

'And George Oaks, the barman,' Sylvia added.

'Oh. Yeah.'

'How did Owen and John get on?' Obviously, they'd heard from Trudy and John himself on this, but Ellie hoped Anna might have something else to add.

Anna spoke in a sad voice. 'They're complete opposites. Owen is Mr Laid Back. John is Mr Type A. He's also the older brother. The whole time I've known Owen, John has been a competitive, jealous nightmare.'

Ellie and Sylvia were listening carefully.

'Owen has never wanted the things John does. He's nowhere near as ambitious and he's also much more content. And I think that made John even more jealous.' She took a sip of tea now, forgetting it was cold.

'Could he have wanted to harm Owen?' Ellie asked. 'Or been capable of it, if they got into a row?' She was thinking about the bust-up that the staff had heard between the two brothers at the pub.

Anna sighed.

Rebus jumped onto the bed and curled up next to Anna.

'I've always said John's temper is dangerous. Owen says I'm exaggerating, and *my* view is he makes excuses for his brother.'

'This is so often the difficulty,' said Ellie. 'People's perceptions differ. How do you get on with Gail?'

'Fine. I have no issue with her. I don't think they're particularly happy but she's loyal. She's OK towards Owen and she's pleasant with me. It's just John I don't like. And I decided a long time ago that life is too short to spend with people I don't like and don't respect.'

'Could you tell us a little bit about how Owen felt about John?'

Anna closed her eyes, as though even thinking about it brought her pain. 'For years, Owen made excuses for his brother and said he deserved pity. He said that no one who was happy behaved the way John did.'

'I agree,' said Sylvia.

'As a yoga teacher, I do too. But Owen continued to spend time with him, to put up with his materialism. I guess it's different when that person is your brother.'

'And the pub?' asked Ellie. 'How did John and Gail come to be managers first of all, then the owners?'

'*Owners?*' She frowned.

'Er ... yes, didn't you know?'

'No. What? They've bought the pub?' She sat up. 'What about Owen?'

Ellie thought about the draft contract papers in their bin downstairs. 'Didn't Owen tell you?'

She shook her head. 'The previous owner, Tom, developed a heart condition–'

'I heard about that.'

'– and he and Maggie decided to get a manager in, so they could retire and enjoy their life together without the stress of the pub.'

'John and Gail.'

She nodded. 'They had a couple of applicants. John and Gail were the obvious choice because they've had lots of experience as publicans. Owen told me Tom and Maggie had decided to sell the place. He said he was interested in buying a share, and had told them so.' She looked at Ellie. 'That was the last I heard. Owen started having meetings, I believe, and I assumed that was about finance.'

'You didn't hear about the row he and John had?'

She shook her head again. 'I don't go into the pub much and Owen stopped talking to me about the place.'

'The staff said they've never seen Owen so angry. It must've been when he found out that John had bought the pub.'

'From underneath him by the sound of it.' Anna shook her head. 'I'm not surprised he was angry. But I don't understand why Owen didn't tell me.'

'Perhaps he was making other arrangements?' Ellie suggested tentatively, to see if Anna knew any more than she was saying.

'We'd agreed to discuss our finances next week. I didn't want him to rush into anything. It was going to be a lot of money.'

Ellie was thinking about the hot air balloon trip. 'I wonder if Owen and John had resolved their differences before the balloon ride?'

'He didn't want to go. I know that.'

That wasn't what Gail had told them.

'But Gail just kept saying, come along, it'll be fine, we'll have a lovely time, bring Anna.'

'Why didn't he just refuse to go?'

'He tried.'

'The morning he left, to go and meet them, did you suggest he didn't go?'

'Yes. He said he'd think about it as he was driving over.'

'So, when John rang you and said Owen hadn't come on the balloon ride, and had gone to McDonald's instead, how did that sit with you?'

'The McDonald's part struck me as weird but when John said Owen had pulled out, I was pleased. I knew Owen was tired so that bit was true, and he said Owen was hungry so McDonald's sort of made sense.' She bit her lip. 'Except – it looks like he didn't go there, and he's disappeared.'

Ellie recounted what the branch manager had told them: Owen hadn't been in.

'Where did he go then?'

'At the moment, we still don't know.' She gave Anna a nod of commitment. 'But we will find out.'

Chapter 24

Downstairs, an hour later, the kitchen was full of laundry bags and baskets of washing again from the water-soaked outhouse. The ironing boards were stacked against the cupboards and the irons were on the worktops.

Ellie and Zoe were staring at the sight in front of them.

'This definitely calls for comfort hot chocolate,' Zoe announced as she dried her hands and reached into the cupboard for the marshmallows. 'Hopefully, Finn will find Brian.'

'I would suggest we have a discussion about this latest development with the body on the beach,' said Ellie.

'I agree,' said Sylvia.

Ellie continued. 'Anna's popped home to get her phone charger, so it's probably a good opportunity.'

While Zoe was making their drinks, Ellie brought up iPlayer on her phone and scrolled back to the news segment they'd watched at 9am. She switched on the subtitles.

'*What we know about the victim is, it's a man in his forties. His ID is known to the police but hasn't been shared. The police are in the process of informing his family. And the circumstances are being treated as suspicious.*'

'So, they think whoever he is, he was murdered,' said Sylvia as she got the biscuit tin out. She spoke quietly. 'Do we think it's going to be Owen?' She looked at Ellie then Zoe. Their faces were as blank as she felt. 'We can't know, can we?'

Ellie shook her head and replied in a similarly quiet voice. 'Being practical, given Owen's missing, I think the chances of it being him *are* increased. But we don't know if there are other missing forty-year-old men that might also fit that description.'

'Don't forget what the police told Anna,' Ellie added. 'Hold on. I made a note of it.' She scrolled through her phone. 'Here we go. When she asked if the body on the beach was Owen's, the police refused to confirm, and said the discovery possibly changes the missing person case. They said they have lines of enquiry they need to pursue.'

'Surely that suggests the two are related somehow?' asked Sylvia.

'I assume so.' Ellie was trying to remember what the police's procedure usually was. When they were certain about an ID, they informed the primary family members. 'What do you make of what Dave said? That they're *in the process of informing the deceased's family.*'

'Hmm,' Sylvia replied. 'Two possibilities. Maybe they are pretty sure about the ID but not certain enough.'

'Yep. That occurred to me too.'

'Or – they can't locate the relatives. I'm sure I remember Ron saying this is more common than people think. For example, if someone is homeless or estranged from people in their family.'

'So, thinking logically,' said Ellie, 'given they haven't told Anna and John that the body *is* Owen's, doesn't that suggest the likelihood is it's not?'

'That would be my reading of the situation too,' said Sylvia. 'But I think we need to be careful about jumping to conclusions. It's fair enough for us to have that as a hypothesis but we can't mention it to anyone else, particularly Anna and John.'

'Agreed,' said Ellie. 'We've checked with Anna that she still wants us to continue investigating Owen's disappearance, and she's confirmed she does, so I suggest we continue doing exactly that.' Ellie spooned melting marshmallow into her mouth.

'I'm sure the police will release the man's ID quickly,' said Sylvia. 'With Owen being local and popular, there's going to be a lot of speculation.'

'I hope the person's ID doesn't get leaked to Katie Douglas at the newspaper. Especially if relatives are still being contacted.' Ellie took a sip of hot chocolate. 'Right. Let's think about what we need to do.'

Chapter 25

The Blixes were still in the kitchen when there was a key in the door. Rebus clattered over.

It was Anna, back again.

'The postman has just delivered a letter from Owen.' Her face was as white as paper. 'Posted in Dover. I've just read it.'

'You're kidding?' said Zoe.

'Nope.' She produced a pale blue envelope from her pocket and took the notepaper out. As she did so, tears welled up in her eyes and she wiped her nose on her sleeve. 'He's gone to the south of France.' The words came out as a squeak.

There was a silence for a few moments.

'To do what?' asked Ellie.

'Crew on someone's yacht as a chef. Cap d'Antibes, near Nice.'

'Really?'

'He posted it presumably before he got on the ferry.'

'Wow.' Zoe's eyes were wide with surprise. 'I wasn't expecting that, were you?'

'No.' Anna handed Ellie the piece of note paper.

Ellie skim-read it for anything Anna may have omitted.

Been invited to work as a chef on a yacht... Want to get out of the village... Once in a lifetime opportunity... Not going to need the car... Really sorry not to tell you to your face... I know it's a bit cowardly... A number of conversations I've been wanting to avoid... Haven't taken my phone...

'Is it Owen's handwriting?'

Anna nodded, tears rolling down her face. 'And he always uses those nylon tip pens and blue ink.' She fixed her gaze on Ellie, blinking thoughtfully. 'Well, I suppose that's the mystery solved. He's gone off on an adventure.' She spluttered, tears coursing down her cheeks. 'But why on earth he wouldn't take his phone is beyond me. And where is it? It's not at home.'

Ellie was trying to decide what to say. 'I'm really sorry.'

'Don't be. At least now I know I don't need to be worried about him. And it's obviously preferable to him having come to harm. I just ...' Her words broke off. She took a tissue from her sleeve and blew her nose. 'I suppose

I hoped he'd gone off somewhere for a day or so and would come home.'

Ellie understood how Anna felt. She knew from Dave's murder cases that in these sorts of situations, not knowing what had happened to loved ones meant a range of things were possible, giving rise to both hope and dread. Finding out the truth gave closure, but it also destroyed all hope.

She put her arm round Anna's shoulders.

'You guys don't need to keep looking for him anymore. I just wish he could have said where he was going, rather than disappearing in the dark and leaving us all worried sick for two days.'

'Do you know what the conversations are that he wanted to avoid?' asked Ellie.

Anna shook her head.

'Perhaps he doesn't mean with you. His brother, maybe, about the pub?'

Anna shrugged. 'Owen hates conflict. He'll do anything he can to avoid it.'

Ellie's brain was throwing up questions. 'He says conversations, *plural*. Can you think who else he might be referring to?'

Anna shook her head again.

'Is it OK to take a quick picture of his note?' Ellie asked her.

'Sure.'

'You need to tell the police you've received this. And show it to them.'

'I will. And I'll tell John, of course, too.'

Ellie recognised the note paper. It was Basildon Bond, from the village shop, if she wasn't mistaken, or a similar make. If Owen had grabbed it up before he left, that suggested he hadn't left on the spur of the moment. The pale paper and hand-writing looked so old fashioned, but then, letter writing was so rare now. It seemed to have been text messages, WhatsApps and emails for so long.

She snapped a picture of Owen's note and the envelope, still trying to take in the news and to process the information it contained. Anna seemed satisfied that the letter was from Owen. And Ellie had no reason to think it wasn't. But she was also aware that it omitted important pieces of information.

Nowhere in it did Owen mention finances, why he'd left his phone behind, how to contact him. It also didn't say when – or *whether* – he was planning to come back.

'So, that's it,' Anna said, biting back tears now. 'I might as well go back home and start getting used to life on my own.'

Ellie caught the hurt in her friend's voice. The yawning chasm of loss.

'Owen hasn't gone missing.' She clasped her hands over her cheeks and nose. 'He's left me.'

—ℓℓℓ—

While Ellie made Anna a mug of tea, Sylvia and Zoe went to check on the outhouse. Sarge and Sean would arrive at some point and would be shocked to see what had happened.

In the kitchen, Ellie discussed with Anna everything she could think of before her friend dashed up to Zoe's room, collected her bag and left, determined to return home now Owen wasn't coming back.

The door closed behind Anna and the house was silent for a few moments until Rebus clacked over to see Ellie. 'Hey, boy.' She crouched down and gave him a hug, hating the idea of Anna being on her own while she felt so abandoned and vulnerable. Then, she texted Zoe saying Anna had left.

'The south of France?' asked Zoe a few minutes later when she and Sylvia returned from the garden.

'Apparently.'

'So, one minute he's leaving her love notes and the next he's legged it to the nearest port and sent her a Dear John letter? It doesn't make sense.' Zoe looked from Ellie to Sylvia.

'And didn't Anna say Owen would never leave her?' said Sylvia.

'It does seem odd,' Ellie agreed.

'She wants us to stand down now and stop looking for Owen,' said Sylvia gently. 'Are we going to?'

'I don't know,' replied Ellie, at a loss for what was best. 'Technically, we started investigating because Anna asked us to. But we can carry on for ourselves if we think there's more to find out. Do we?'

'She said she's sure it's Owen's handwriting, didn't she?' asked Sylvia.

Ellie nodded. 'She's convinced it's from him. And it might be, but it doesn't mean he's gone where he says.'

'That's a good point,' said Sylvia. 'The letter might be a cover.'

'I wonder what John will make of this.' Ellie started tidying. 'He's convinced Owen went to meet a business associate.'

'The whole thing's as weird as heck,' said Zoe. 'I think we should carry on investigating.' She searched her mum's face for agreement.

'Gran?' asked Zoe.

Sylvia was shaking her head. 'One minute Anna's adamant something's happened to Owen. Now she's convinced by a lame note. Something isn't right. I think we should carry on.'

Zoe let out a whoop.

There was a rap at the door.

'Can't be Sarge,' Ellie shouted over Rebus' barks. 'He goes through the gate to the garden.'

Zoe went to see who it was.

'Alright darlin',' said a delivery driver, as he patted a tumble dryer on a trolley. Behind him was another machine. 'OK to leave them here?'

Chapter 26

Ellie had just got into the jeep when her phone rang. It was a mobile number, not one from her contacts. 'Ellie Blix. How can I help?'

'Ellie, it's Gail Field here.' Her tone was brisk. 'There's something I haven't told you which you need to know. Could we meet?'

'Sure. When were you thinking?'

'How about now? On the green by the pond?'

'Sure. Is it OK to bring Zoe? She can have a look at the doorbell app on your phone while we chat.'

Ten minutes later, Gail and Ellie were sitting on the bench at the duck pond.

Zoe had Rebus off the lead. While he was sniffing round the bonfire, tracking scents and squealing, she was looking at Gail's phone.

Finn and his tree-surgeon boss, Bob Campbell, were depositing timber and branches on the enormous pile from Bob's pickup.

'I didn't mention it when we spoke,' said Gail in a low voice, 'because it felt gossipy.' She was in jeans, ankle boots, a polo neck jumper and a padded gilet with a hood.

'Thanks for ringing. We need to know everything that's potentially relevant.' Ellie was still thinking about the letter Anna had received from Owen. 'Unfortunately, a lot of important information often is gossip.'

'It's about Anna. I've always got on well with her and Owen, and everyone knows they have a good relationship. But I don't think she's been in love with him for some time and...' Her sentence petered out.

Ellie had a feeling she knew what was coming.

'She's been having an affair for a while now.'

'How long's a while?'

'A year? Maybe more. It feels gossipy to say so, but the information itself isn't hearsay or gossip. I "caught" her with the person concerned in ... let's just call it "a compromising situation".'

'Will you give me the person's name?'

'No, I'm going to leave Anna to do that. She'll be annoyed enough about me disclosing the affair, so I'll let her complete the details. All I will say is that I don't think she could have picked a more unsuitable person.'

Ellie's ears pricked up at this.

'Got him,' Zoe shouted, waving Gail's mobile phone. 'He put the gnome outside your house at 3am on Monday morning.'

'It will have been dark,' said Gail. 'How good's the image?'

'Excellent. You've got a light on a motion sensor.' She passed Ellie the phone. 'Tall, well-built, dark clothes, balaclava. I've copied a bit of the video and emailed it to myself. Hope that's OK.'

Ellie showed Gail the image. 'Recognise him?'

'No. Don't like the balaclava at all. And why's he targeting us? We've only just moved here.'

'No idea. My family too. Anna and Owen. The grave. No obvious pattern.' She shrugged. 'Anyway – back to the encounter with Anna and her *paramour*. Where was this?'

Zoe sat next to her mum and listened to the end of the conversation.

'In Appledown Woods. I was having a walk. The person concerned camps in the woods sometimes.'

'*Camps?*'

'Yes. He's got one of those round tents. And whenever anyone complains about him being there, he just packs up his tent and pitches it somewhere else.'

Chapter 27

While Zoe went to do a cleaning job, Ellie was at Tollgate Cottage, upstairs in Anna's bedroom.

'Anna, I've been talking to Gail.' She had to shout over the ABBA that was blasting out.

The windows were open, and Anna was up a rickety wooden ladder, taking the curtains down. A vacuum cleaner was on the floor with a black bin liner.

'She said she needed to add something important to what she told us. Something ... *delicate.*'

'It doesn't matter,' Anna replied. 'It's over and Owen's not coming back.'

Despite the loud music and frantic activity, Ellie caught the brittleness in her friend's voice. 'You know what it's about though, don't you?'

Anna nodded. 'I asked her not to tell anyone.' She chucked one curtain on the carpet and leaned over on the ladder to start on the other side.

Ellie took hold of the ladder with both hands. 'I don't think she has done, but you can talk to her about that. I didn't sense any ulterior motive in her telling me. I think she simply thought we should know.' She was wondering why Anna was acting like it wasn't a big thing.

'Did she tell you who the person was?' Anna started to cry, and the ladder was wobbling.

Ellie noticed Anna had used the past tense. 'No. She … Look, I'm worried you're going to fall.' She wedged her foot on the bottom rung. 'Could you … er … come down?' She wanted to suggest the music volume was lowered but it was Anna's safety that worried her most.

'I'll be fine,' Anna replied, sniffing. 'I want to get this done. Change the energy in this place.' She tugged at one of the curtain hooks and it pinged across the room. 'His name is Todd Reynolds, if you want to know,' she blurted. 'We were going to get married.'

More past tense.

'Todd who works for John at the pub?'

They were still having to shout over the music.

'Yup.'

'Was that why you stopped going in there?'

'Who said that?'

'One of the staff.'

Trudy had said it coincided with John taking the place over.

'Mainly that, yes.'

'Look, I'm not here to judge. You asked us to help find Owen and that's what I'm focussing on here.'

'Well, he's gone. He's in France. I've told you. There's no need to bother now.'

Ellie wasn't sure whether Anna genuinely believed this or whether it was simply preferable to thinking he was dead. She would leave it for now. 'Gail said something about Todd living in a–'

'... tent.' Anna nodded. 'Yes. Some of the time. He didn't believe in home ownership and property. His mother has a house, but it's half-derelict and he doesn't live there except when it's freezing.'

Cora. Cora Reynolds. The Old Hare and Hounds. The house which, as kids, they'd always thought was haunted.

'We always thought Todd's name was Mickey Reynolds. Isn't he a poacher?' As teenagers, he'd had the reputation of stealing and swindling people, and they'd nicknamed him Mickey, as in 'take the mickey'.

Anna stopped what she was doing. Her eyes filled with tears. 'He's not a poacher. He just lived an unconventional lifestyle and liked being amongst nature.'

'Anna, why do you keep talking about him in the past tense?'

'Because I *think he's dead*,' she spluttered. 'He texted me on Sunday evening, saying he was meeting someone at the end of the pier.'

Ellie had a sinking feeling in her stomach. 'Oh, no. You mean the body on the beach?'

Anna nodded.

'Look, please come down and can we get this music off? I can't think.'

Anna climbed down the ladder and faced Ellie. 'I'm sure it's Todd. He had a couple of things to collect from me and said he'd call me straight after the meeting. But I never heard from him, and his phone has gone straight to voicemail ever since Sunday evening.'

Ellie was trying to decide what this information meant. 'Who was he going to meet?'

'I don't know. He didn't say. It wasn't just an affair, Ells. I know no-one in the village likes him, but they didn't know him like I did. We were in love. I was going to leave Owen, get a divorce, and Todd and I were going to go away together and get married.'

Ellie led Anna round the pile of curtains and over to the bed. They both sat down. 'Erm ... OK,' said Ellie.

'I've known him for years. When we were teenagers, we went out together. He was my first boyfriend. But my parents hated him and weren't keen on Cora. They said she's a witch.'

Ellie knew a few people held a similar view. 'This changes everything. You do realise that, don't you?' She and Anna looked at each other.

'I know.'

'Do you really believe Owen's in France on a yacht?'

'I don't know.' A sob burst from Anna's mouth. 'I'm scared, Ells.'

'Sweetheart.' Ellie had sensed this was what the clear out was about. Doing something rather than nothing. She took hold of Anna's hands, clasping them in hers. 'A day at a time. Let's find out what's happened to both of them, yes?'

'OK,' Anna whispered.

'Do you know where Owen is?'

She shook her head emphatically. 'No. I would have said.'

'Do you know who went up in the hot air balloon?'

'No.'

'When did you last speak to Todd?'

'Friday night. Before the balloon ride.'

'Did Owen know about your affair?'

'Not that I know of. I have a feeling Gail might have told John though.' She hesitated, as though there was something else she wanted to say. 'But – I'd broken it off with Todd. Two weeks ago.' She sniffed. 'It was *everything,* and now it's all over and I'm sure he's dead.'

Chapter 28

'See if you can turn your sleuthing eyes to this CCTV, can you?' Reverend Jackson said to Sylvia, who he'd invited round for afternoon tea. 'I've promised Mrs Blackman I'll find out who's nicked the gnome from her husband's grave.'

They were in the Rectory office, a sumptuous room with an inglenook fireplace and stone surround. Logs crackled in the basket and a warm orange glow reflected round the room.

'He was a gnome enthusiast all his life, you know, and specifically requested a gnome on his grave, in his will.'

Sylvia managed to stop herself from making a sneery remark. She'd never been a fan of gnomes or seen their attraction.

'I know some people aren't keen on them,' Reverend Jackson continued, 'but others see them as protectors who guard sacred places. Their Scandinavian folklore origins might not seem very church-y, but they hark back to ancient Rome where statues guarded against evil spirits.'

'Actually,' Sylvia replied, 'now you mention it, we had a talk about gnomes at the Women's Institute a while back. I'm sure the lady said they're seen by many as symbols of good luck. Aren't they used to watch over crops and livestock in some areas?'

'That's right. Farmers tuck them away in barns. People have them at home for the same reasons. Protection and luck.' He beamed at her, as though he was thrilled to be discussing a subject he was interested in. 'Shall we get stuck into this CCTV?'

'I might have guessed there was a hidden agenda to you inviting me round,' she teased. 'How much is there?' She was on first name terms with the vicar now.

Leonard.

'Call me, Len,' he'd told her in the Rattling Cat the other night, after the second glass of Sauvignon Blanc.

'Twelve hours, I'm afraid. But Gladys' grandson, Ewan, has narrowed the time down.'

'Thank goodness for that. I've got bell-ringing practice this evening and my job at the charity shop in the morning.'

Leonard carried on. 'Ewan put a new gnome on his grandad's grave on Saturday, just before dark. It had gone by the morning.' He heaved the solid wood desk towards the fire with a grunt. 'I'll get you a chair.'

It was a long time since Sylvia had seen CCTV. Before he retired, Ron would occasionally look at it on his laptop. This was much better quality though. Clearer. Less grainy.

Leonard – she couldn't call him Len; it was too much like Ron – placed a high-backed dining chair for her. She got comfy on it and nudged her shoes off to warm her feet by the fire. She could get used to this.

Leonard pointed at the screen. 'There's Ewan, look, with his dad, putting the new gnome down with fresh, yellow dahlias.' He pressed a few computer keys. 'Then, just over twelve hours later, the flowers are still there but the gnome's gone.'

It was true. The gnome had disappeared.

'I can't sit here for twelve hours. Is there a way to speed up the viewing? My granddaughter does that on YouTube sometimes when she wants the highlights.'

'Ah. I've just seen that setting. Now, where was it?' He clicked a few more times. 'There we are. What shall I select? Triple speed?'

'Let's try that. See what turns up. We can always go back to the start on double speed if that's too fast.'

'I tried your lemon curd sponge recipe, by the way.' He glowed with pride. 'Would you like a slice? I'd be interested to know what you think of the consistency and flavour. I made a couple of strategic changes.'

'Lovely. Thank you.' Sylvia was rather enjoying being waited on. And it made a nice change not being the one who did all the baking.

'You keep your eyes peeled on the monitor. I'm determined to catch the blighter.' He scuttled off.

St Mary's had a pretty graveyard. Brick and flint church. Couple of lovely old yew trees. Benches. A mixture of gravestone styles. A few tombs. Sylvia could almost smell the damp leaves and earth. Feel the pine cones beneath her feet. Hear the cries of the magpies and foxes.

A rabbit hopped into view, disappearing quickly. Then two more, their stubby tails flashing white as they lolloped.

Leonard returned with a pot of tea on a tray, with two cups and saucers, a jug of milk, a pot of sugar lumps, and two generous slices of cake on china plates with a posh cake fork each.

Sylvia did like a healthy slice. Nothing worse than a mingy helping and having to ask for seconds, worrying you'd be thought greedy.

They settled down companionably, chatting about the Rectory, Leonard's temporary position here, the village, the recent disappearances and – inevitably – the suspicious death of the man whose body had just washed up on the beach.

'I'm sure you and your family will have it solved in no time. I'll never forget how prompt you were with that poor man who was shot with an arrow in the bluebell woods.'

'That's very kind.'

It was through a Blix Blitz investigation that she'd met Leonard.

'How's the cake?' he asked, peering at her eagerly.

'Delicious. I'm sensing you added extra lemon, did you?'

'Well detected. Yes, a bit of peel to add to the tartness. And a smidgeon of ground clove.'

Sylvia was finding it tricky to keep her eyes on the CCTV monitor *and* get forkfuls of cake safely into her mouth, but hopefully any lapses *she* had wouldn't coincide with Leonard's.

The camera focus shifted briefly, and Sylvia saw the area of the graveyard where, back in the summer, she'd bumped into her estranged mother. How long ago that seemed now. How different life had been since then too, getting to know her again. Dave, getting to know the grandmother he didn't remember. Zoe, getting to know the great-grandmother she'd never even heard of.

Then the camera switched back to the side of the church where Mr Blackman's grave was. A man came into view, pushing a wheelbarrow. Sturdy frame. Green woolly hat, beige jacket with pockets.

'What's he got in there?' Sylvia asked. 'Manure? Or gravel for the path?' Her eyes began to focus.

'Hold on. What's he doing?' Leonard sat up. 'Is that a–?'

Sylvia peered closer. Screamed. 'Leonard! It's a *body*. He's got a body in that–'

'By Jove, you're right.' He paused the footage. Clicked back one frame at a time.

Legs hanging over the front from the knee down.

Navy blue trainers. Red jumper.

One arm dangling on the ground.

'What the heck's he doing with a body in there?' Leonard let the tape play again. 'Who are they both?'

The man wheeled the body along the path, across the grass towards a tomb. He did a quick three-sixty scan of the area and beckoned to someone off camera. Pulled a crowbar out of the barrow, slid it under the top of the tomb ...

'No, no, no,' shouted Leonard, as though it was happening in real time. 'That's desecration. You can't do that.'

A third man had arrived now, and together they eased up the stone top of the tomb.

Sylvia grabbed her phone from her bag on the floor. 'We need to call the police. *Now.*'

Chapter 29

'Ellie. I wanted to speak to you about your Christmas order. We're trialling some new sausages this year and ...' Nick Matthews stopped mid-sentence. 'Ah. You haven't come to talk about meat, have you?'

Ellie had known Nick since they were at school. He had run Matthews' butchers all his adult life, and for the last five years with his son, Charlie.

'I'm afraid not, but I will take some of your delicious lamb mince with me when I go. Sylvia's been muttering for days about a new shepherd's pie recipe she's devised.'

Although it was 3pm, the shop was, as usual, still busy. Locals stood at the counter, eyeing up the freshly cut meat in the chiller cabinets. Behind the counter, facing the customers, someone had written on the chalk board: ALL OUR PRODUCE IS ETHICALLY SOURCED FROM LOCAL SUPPLIERS. Ellie hadn't noticed it before. It reminded her of Trudy's comments about Nick challenging John Field on his game sources.

Nick leaned towards the back of the shop. 'Ross, do you want to come into the front while I talk to Mrs Blix?' He turned to Ellie, wiping his hands on a cloth. 'We've a young lad on work experience. Come through to the back.'

Charlie took over Ross' supervision. 'I'll take the money, and do the till and the change,' he told him patiently. 'You take the orders and weigh up the meat. That OK, buddy? Put your gloves on ...'

Ellie followed Nick, who was striding ahead in his white butcher's coat and boots.

'I'm assuming this is about Owen's disappearance, is it?'

'Actually, it's about Todd Reynolds.'

'Todd?' His face clouded over. 'Why are you asking about him? He's not popular. You know he's a poacher, don't you?'

'So we've been told. What do you know about him?'

'That he's a right scallywag, that's what. He's poached rabbits with ferrets for years. We've all known about it. But the word is, he's been shooting deer again in the woods at night.'

'Ah.'

'It's an absolute no, Ellie.' His jaw tightened as he spoke. 'Against the law, not fair on the animals, and it doesn't go down well round here.' He washed his hands in the stainless- steel sink. 'For a number of years now, Todd's tried to sell poached game to the pubs, restaurants and even some of the traders. Even out of season. The man's got no morals and no shame. You tell him no; he turns up again the next week with something else.'

'Has he offered you meat?'

'Not for a long time because he knows I'm not interested. He kept trying with the Windmill Inn. Fortunately, Owen had more sense. Sent him packing, just like we did. But that brother of Owen's, John, he's a different story.' His eyes narrowed.

Ellie was all ears.

'They've got history, those two; John and Todd. I don't know what it is but it's bad news. Not just for the hospitality industry but for the village too.' He dried his hands. 'Poaching isn't just about cheating land owners. There are health implications too. You need to know how to shoot game, and how to store and transport it. Otherwise, it has an increased risk of food poisoning.'

'Oh crikey.'

'Owen's up to speed on all that. Steered clear. Dave knows about Todd's activities. It's not his area, of course, but he's been after Todd Reynolds for a while now.'

This was news to Ellie. 'Have you had any dealings with John Field?'

'I was just about to mention him. Yes and no. Before Christmas last year, a new meat supplier started up. Long story short, it was John and Todd. The paperwork wasn't right, so we weren't interested, and that was before I learnt Todd was involved. There was a lot of talk at the time about some of it being poached meat.'

'Wow. So, John was not just buying it but selling it too.'

'Yes. What was strange was that almost as soon as the supplier started up, it disappeared. It was as though John realised he wasn't going to get away with flogging dodgy meat.'

'Did Owen have any involvement in that?'

Nick shook his head. 'He heard what was going on, and he kept out of it. But I overheard him having a screaming row with John one day about his intention to move to Lower Wootton.'

'Really? Saying what?'

'Owen told John in no uncertain terms not to come here. He said he didn't want John ruining things for him and for the village.'

Ellie shuddered. 'That's almost prophetic.' As chilling as Nick's words were, they also weren't a complete surprise. But it nevertheless shocked Ellie to know there was such strength of feeling between the two brothers. 'So, John and Todd are involved with illegal meat.' Ellie remembered George's bicycle outside the pub. 'Is George Oaks in on this too?'

'I'd imagine so. There's a reason John brought some of his staff over from their Canterbury pub.'

Nick bagged up some lamb mince for Ellie and a bone for Rebus. 'Anyway – let's change the subject before my blood pressure explodes. Are you all going to the firework display on Thursday? How has November come round so quickly?'

They chatted about the village. Halloween. Guy Fawkes' Night.

'By the way, I had a pint with Dave the other day.' Nick's words were tentative.

'Oh, right.' Ellie felt a ripple of nausea. Was he going to say Dave had decided to take the job in Birmingham?

'He mentioned a promotion in the Midlands.'

'Yes, he told us yesterday. I don't know the details though and hadn't realised it's a promotion for him. He was just about to fill us in and got called out.'

'Do you *want* him to leave the village?'

'No-o.' Ellie froze for a moment. She didn't mind Nick's questions. But answering was a different matter. 'It's his life though. If he wants a fresh start, a challenge, I understand that. We aren't a couple anymore.'

Nick pulled a mock-impatient face. 'Come on, Ells. We've all known each other since we were kids.'

Ellie nodded. Not being a couple anymore was one thing. She still saw Dave around the village. But if he moved away, all that would change.

'You know he wants you guys to get back together. *Everyone in the village* knows that.'

Nick's words prompted a surge of longing.

And then, as usual, the fear closed in; the memory, as clear and visceral as it had been at the time, of how much Dave's affair had hurt her.

Chapter 30

While Sylvia and Leonard were waiting for the police to arrive at the Rectory, they put the time to good use.

'It would be helpful to have another look at the CCTV,' Sylvia told him. 'The sections with the wheelbarrow and the tomb. See if we can identify the people involved.'

'You're welcome to do so. Whatever might help.'

'The police will take it to analyse.' She had an idea. 'If I can get Zoe to help me, would you mind if I copied it?'

'No problem. I wish I knew how to do it, but my IT skills are sadly lacking.'

'Hopefully, I can get Zoe to help me find the bit where the gnome is taken too.'

'Oh, please. That would be kind.'

Within a few minutes, Sylvia was on the phone to Zoe. She put the phone on loudspeaker so Leonard could hear too.

'You'll need your glasses and a USB stick, Gran.'

'Cheeky mare.'

'I've got a USB stick for my laptop,' said Leonard. 'Hold on, I'll go and get it. I was using it for my sermons before I learnt about cloud storage.' He shuffled out of the room.

Sylvia filled Zoe in on what they'd seen on the CCTV.

'They put the body in a tomb?' Zoe screeched. 'No way. That's like a horror movie.'

'Quite. But an ingenious idea, if you think about it. Bodies in water float after a while. Buried bodies get found by dogs. Who's going to look for a dead body in a place where there already is one?'

'They will if the culprits get caught on CCTV,' said Zoe. 'I've only just switched the CCTV back on at St Mary's. What's the bet the blokes who dumped the body in the tomb didn't know that? They'll be stuffed now. Someone's bound to recognise them.'

Leonard was back, brandishing a shiny USB stick. 'Practically new. I've copied my sermons on Luke and sinners, and Colossians and tolerance, into the Cloud.'

'OK, Gran, I need you to listen. Put the USB stick into the USB port on the DVR.'

'... on the what?' Technology phobia gripped Sylvia and she heard the shriek in her voice. She took a deep breath.

You can do this. Come on. You've got to.

Chapter 31

V ery quickly, the police had the churchyard cordoned off and a forensics tent over the tomb. Crime scene investigators were doing a sweep of the graveyard.

Poor Reverend Jackson was traumatised by what he'd seen and was receiving medical attention from the paramedics.

Sarge and his nephew, who looked after the graves and cut the grass, were being questioned.

Once the police had spoken to her, Sylvia said goodbye to Leonard and headed home with the USB stick safely in her bag. Past a pumpkin lantern outside the Rectory. Past the banner on the railings, advertising the village bonfire and fireworks on Thursday evening.

She turned into the path beside the church. It wasn't completely dark yet, and Pennypot Lane wasn't what she called 'country dark'. It had street lights along it, and some of the lighting from the houses added to the illumination. However, it had spooked her, seeing first the body in the wheelbarrow, and then the two men bundle the poor chap into the tomb before replacing the lid. It had seemed unreal. But what made the CCTV particularly chilling was that it *wasn't* a TV drama. It was a recording of what had *actually* happened.

Neither she nor Leonard had recognised any of the three men. The police would hopefully identify them quickly. They had both agreed the man pushing the wheelbarrow had looked sturdy.

But what did that mean exactly?

Strong?

Muscular?

Chunky?

She knew from experience it wasn't too hard to push something heavy in a wheelbarrow – she'd done it in the garden with Ron several times – but getting heavy items in and out was a different proposition. She'd always left that to Ron.

OK, the chap pushing the wheelbarrow had had help, but he'd done most of the lifting. He'd been able to lift the body *and* move the heavy stone on the top of the tomb. That took considerable strength and stamina. In contrast, it had looked as if the man *in* the wheelbarrow had a slighter frame than the man pushing it.

What a strange case this was turning out to be. Sprawling and shocking – and different. On all their previous investigations, they'd started with a dead body. This time it had taken two days for one to turn up.

Behind Sylvia, the blue lights of the emergency services sliced through the sky. She caught the yellow of an ambulance as it flashed past the end of the lane towards the church.

Her thoughts ran to Anna and her conviction that Owen's letter was genuine. It would soon be on the internet – and the village grapevine – that the police were at the church with crime scene officers, and that someone else had been found dead in their sleepy, usually safe village.

When Sylvia arrived home, Zoe was in the kitchen with Finn and Ellie. Rebus and Mouse were chasing each other round the windmill.

'You've been ages,' said Zoe. 'Have you got the Rev's USB?'

'Hello, Gran,' said Sylvia, her voice sarcastic. 'So pleased you're back. Are you OK?'

'Sorry. You alright?'

'I will be. Here you go.' She passed it to Zoe, who plugged it straight into her laptop.

'On there is the CCTV of the men disposing of the body–'

'I can't believe they opened a tomb,' said Ellie, 'and put a man's body inside. That's gross.'

'Isn't it? And somewhere there will be footage of the gnome being stolen, too. If you could find that, Leonard would be very grateful.'

'Will do. Your boyfriend's done Blix Investigators a huge favour, Gran, asking you to help him with the church CC–.'

'Hang on,' Sylvia said, stopping in her tracks. 'Wasn't there a description of Owen Field in Anna's Facebook post? I'm sure I remember something about trainers.'

Zoe took her phone out of her skirt pocket, swiped the screen and opened Facebook. Made a couple of clicks. 'Here we go.' She scanned the post for the right spot. *'Owen Field. Last seen wearing a navy coat, black jeans, blue Nike trainers and a red jumper.'*

Sylvia pulled out a chair at the table and sat down with a thump. 'Unless someone else with a red jumper and blue trainers has been killed, I'd say the body in the wheelbarrow is Owen's.'

Chapter 32

After a medicinal brandy on the sofa, Sylvia managed to marshal her thoughts. 'We'll have to wait for the police to speak to Anna. We can't interfere with their procedures.'

Ellie and Zoe were on the sofa opposite. Zoe had her laptop on her knees and was still scouring the CCTV footage.

'Plus – it wouldn't be kind to tell her that another body has been found, and make her worry,' added Ellie. 'And it's not our place to tell her we think the body is Owen's until the police have confirmed it is.'

Ellie checked her emails to see when Brian was coming to install their new consumer unit and fix the wiring in the outhouse. She then started checking the Facebook groups for replies and comments.

'Perhaps your boyfriend needs to join Blix Investigators, Gran,' said Zoe.

Sylvia was pretending she hadn't heard Zoe. It was the second time in a few minutes she'd made this joke and Sylvia was feeling tired and cranky.

'Do you suppose that's because he doesn't know many people round here yet?' Zoe continued.

'Oh. Are you talking to me?' asked Sylvia, staring into the distance nonchalantly. 'I didn't hear anything interesting.'

'Isn't it funny how you kept teasing me about Jake Campbell only a few months ago,' said Ellie, 'and calling him my "boyfriend" when he wasn't, but you don't like us joking about Reverend Jackson?'

Sylvia wasn't in the mood for jokes, and she didn't want to talk about Leonard. Seeing photos of Ron on Facebook had stirred her up and guilt was tugging at her.

'Here we are,' said Zoe. 'What's this? Man entering the graveyard at 0245 hours. Glances round. That looks a bit suss.'

Ellie leaned over so she could see the footage.

'Dark clothes,' said Zoe. 'Beanie. Heads straight for Mr Blackman's grave. Looks round again. Takes a bin liner out of his pocket and–'

'... grabs the gnome. In the bag and off. What a scumbag.' Ellie was indignant.

Zoe pressed pause on the video. 'So, that's him. I'll enhance the resolution and get some enlarged images. Compare those with the ones from Gail's doorbell video. See if we can identify him.'

'Well done, lovey.' Ellie gave Zoe a hug. 'I couldn't do any of this technology stuff.'

'I'll ring Leonard shortly,' said Sylvia. 'Give him the news. Going back to the person in the wheelbarrow – if it's Owen Field, who do we think the other two men are?'

'I've been thinking about that,' Zoe said quietly. 'The guy pushing it is tall and muscular and wears a green, woolly hat and a beige coat. Who do we know that fits the bill?'

They all shrugged.

'This case is truly infuriating,' said Sylvia.

She saw Ellie and Zoe exchange looks.

'Nothing from Brian. I'll have to ring him.' Ellie switched to her laptop. 'I find it easy on my phone to miss replies on Facebook. I've logged into the running group that you and Finn posted in. It's really busy. People asking about supplements, protein shakes, muscle rub, discount codes on trainers, treadmill maintenance ... It's a whole new language.'

'Let's have a look.' Zoe leaned over to see the screen. 'Hmm. Quite a lot of people are looking for running partners. Oh, look. There's one here from George from the pub about training for the half marathon.'

'He mentioned that to me yesterday.'

'What does his post say?' Sylvia asked.

'He goes out Monday, Wednesday and Saturday mornings at 6am.'

'How can he have been helping John and Gail to inflate their balloon then if he was out running first thing Saturday morning?' asked Sylvia. 'Does he mention going later that day?'

Zoe traced the comments down the laptop screen. 'No. Someone's asked him if he was going out on Saturday, and he said yes. They arranged to meet at Deal pier at 6am.'

'Perhaps he wasn't feeling well and cancelled?' said Ellie. 'We'll have to check with him.'

'Hmm,' said Sylvia. 'I doubt that somehow. Gail and John would've needed to have the balloon crew firmly in place, even if it's just one person. They wouldn't have been able to wait until the last minute to find out if George was available.'

'OK, well, let's not jump to conclusions,' replied Ellie. 'Let's speak to him and see what he has to say. What else have we got? Anything interesting?'

'I'm looking in the anglers' group,' Zoe continued. 'There's a lot of chat – full of speculation, of course – about whose the body is on the beach.'

'I saw that earlier,' said Ellie. 'Actually – that reminds me. I haven't told you about Anna.' She filled them in on the affair.

'She was going to leave Owen,' Zoe summarised, 'then called it all off and now thinks the dead man on the beach is Todd?'

'Good grief,' said Sylvia. 'Anyone in the angling group mention Todd's name?'

'No,' replied Zoe. 'It's mainly all memes, stupid jokes and crass comments.'

'Sounds about right,' Sylvia muttered from the sofa.

Zoe continued feeding back. 'There's a post from Katie Douglas at the newspaper. Put up first thing this morning and asking for information from anyone who was on the beach on Saturday night. And ... wait. Someone's asking about the gnome on the pier.'

'Really?'

'A chap called Gary says he saw a bloke put it in place on the pier last night and lean over to take a pic of the gnome on his phone.'

'Screenshot his details, will you?' said Ellie.

'Young-ish man in dark clothes and a balaclava, according to Gary.'

They all looked at each other.

Zoe spoke first. 'Gotta be the same guy as in the grave-yard, surely?'

Chapter 33

It was almost dark when Ellie and Zoe got out of the jeep at Hawking Down. It was one of Ellie's favourite places for walking and thinking. Up high, with a vast plateau which was a disused World War I airfield, the day-light views went on for miles. Tonight, the sky was clear, and views stretched over the channel and towards Kings-down to the right. In the semi-dark, ship lights twinkled.

While Sylvia was having a nap on the sofa, Ellie wanted to think. To allow her thoughts to run free so she could clear her mind and make decisions.

Owen's disappearance was playing on her mind, and she was worried about Anna. It was the same dilemma she'd experienced before with Blix Investigators. Many of the people involved with their cases were her friends; people she socialised with and cared about. And Anna was more than her yoga instructor. Owen was more than the chef in the local pub. It was bad enough thinking that a tragic accident might have befallen him, but it was much tougher now it looked as though somebody had not just hurt him deliberately – but killed him and dumped his body.

She was also confused about Dave – what to say and do about his job offer in Birmingham.

Zoe opened the jeep hatch and released Rebus and Agatha – who they'd collected from Dave's flat. The two dogs leaped into the undergrowth around the trees on the bank up to Hawking Down, squealing and whining, tails like propellers, the lights on their collars flashing in the dark.

Ellie jumped after them, recognising the familiar sound. 'Someone's either dumped food,' she told Zoe, 'or there's something stinky in there they want to roll in.'

'Probably a fox,' replied Zoe.

'It's food. Someone's dumped a rucksack with food in it.'

'Oh, yuck. The foxes will soon eat it. There's an ancient bicycle over here too with a wooden box on the back rack.'

'What sort of box?' said Ellie, peering into the under-growth. 'Hold on. I'm sure that's the bike I saw outside the Windmill Inn. It didn't have the box on the back then, though.'

'Whose is it?'

Ellie shrugged. 'I assumed it was George's, but that box is for ferrets. It must belong to Todd Reynolds. What's it doing here?' She took a snap of it with her phone.

Once on the chalky grassland, Rebus and Agatha chased each other, wrestled and play-fought, relishing their freedom. Ellie smiled as she watched Zoe chasing them now, her plaits flapping, the fluorescent strips flashing on her jacket.

'Don't go too far, Zo,' Ellie shouted. 'If they see – or smell – a rabbit, they'll be off.'

After a few minutes, Zoe returned with the dogs. She gave Rebus and Agatha a treat and she and Ellie sat on the bench to admire the lights in the Channel.

Ellie was pulling burrs out of the fur on Agatha's ears when her phone dinged with a Google alert notification. She'd had several in the last twenty-four hours, media outlets covering Owen's disappearance, so she opened her email expecting another but when she clicked on the article and scanned the contents, it wasn't. 'Missing person appeal in the local newspaper,' she told Zoe. 'Created by Katie Douglas.'

Hearing the chief reporter's name made Ellie's jaw clench. The Blixes had discovered a year earlier that the paper's editor had contacts in the police – and allied services – who leaked information to him.

'Who?'

Ellie scanned the piece for the gist. *'Todd Reynolds, forty-three–'*

'Oh, no.' Zoe covered her face with her hands. 'You said Anna is convinced the body on the beach is Todd's.'

'This suggests it's not just her who suspects he might have come to harm.' Ellie carried on reading aloud. *'Male, six foot. Reported missing by his mother. Small teardrop tattoo on his left cheek. Last seen on Sunday evening, going out to meet some friends for a drink.'*

This was awful. First Owen had gone missing and was dead.

Now a second person was missing, also linked to the village pub.

What was going on?

'Do you think Anna's right?' Zoe's voice was a whisper.

'No idea. I know very little about him. He's certainly got some enemies. C'mon. Let's get the dogs in the jeep. We can read the appeal properly without freezing.' She was thinking of Anna, and hoping she wasn't on her own.

Ellie and Zoe bundled the dogs across the grass, back down the track and into the jeep. They climbed in themselves and read the article in full.

'One of Katie's usual click-bait-y headlines too,' said Ellie. '"An epidemic of missing people in Wootton"? What a cow that woman is. It's so insulting to the victims' families.'

'Dad's going to be furious,' said Zoe. 'She's been on his hit-list ever since she called him the village lothario.'

Ellie groaned. 'I think it would be useful to have another word with Trudy at the pub. But we'd better wait 'til the police finish at the church and confirm this chap's disappearance. And I'd better tell the police about the dumped bike.'

'Also, if the body on the beach is Todd's,' Zoe added, 'they'll need to notify his mother.' She paused. 'So much for a missing person case. It now looks like there have been two suspicious deaths.'

'Please may there not be any more,' said Ellie, teeth gritted. She started up the engine and switched the heater on.

Zoe cleared her throat. 'Changing the subject: before we came out, I was checking current protocols for hot air balloon rides in the UK. They're different depending on whether the balloon is taken up as part of a commercial operation, offering services to the public, or whether it's a personal flight by a pilot who owns his own balloon.'

'What have you found out?'

'I was hoping there would be a requirement for all pilots to state who their passengers are but that's not the case.

Commercial operators must do this, but not private pilots.'

'So, we have no way of verifying who actually went up in that balloon the other morning?'

'Nope. But there aren't an infinite amount of possibilities. I'm trying to find someone who knows about balloon flying, who can fill us in on the logistics of taking off, flying and landing.'

'That's a good idea. Definitely worth finding an expert.'

'Hold on. Didn't Dad do a balloon ride with Pete, Nick and Bob for their fortieth birthdays?'

'Oh, yes. That's right. They did. Bob organised it.' Ellie swiped her phone screen. 'He'll know who the pilot was. Hopefully he'll be able to help us.'

Chapter 34

When Ellie and Zoe got home, Anna was waiting for them, a tiny ball on the doorstep.

She got up when she saw them and ran to Ellie. She had her dressing gown over the top of pyjamas and slippers. 'The police have told me about Owen's body being put in the tomb.' Her face was streaked with tears, blotchy and mascara-smeared. 'And Jaq told me about the piece in the local paper about Todd being missing.'

'Oh, love. We're so sorry.'

Zoe was holding the dogs.

'It seems you might have been right about the yacht,' said Anna sadly.

'I suppose he could've been intending to go,' Zoe suggested. 'Wrote that note and was intercepted before he left England. Or someone else wrote the note hoping it would throw us off the scent.'

Anna sniffed and blew her nose. 'The main thing is we've finally found him and can lay him to rest. The thought of him in a tomb with...' She went even paler.

Ellie nodded.

'He was a good, kind man. He didn't deserve this.'

'Of course not. Come in.' She put her key in the door. 'Let's get into the warm. Make you a cup of sweet tea before you keel over.'

Zoe followed them in with Rebus and Agatha.

'You have told the police about your relationship with Todd, haven't you?' Ellie took her coat off and hung it up. She led Anna into the lounge, where Rebus and Agatha were jumping over Sylvia. The TV was on low.

'Yes, I have,' said Anna. 'I told Dave everything when he informed me of Owen's death.'

Ellie's thoughts were scrambled. 'Does Todd own a green woolly hat and a beige coat?'

'Not as far as I know. I can't imagine him wearing either of those things, to be honest.'

'How did Owen and Todd get on?'

'Owen had no time for Todd.'

'Is that because Todd was – I know you don't like the word but – a poacher?'

'I don't like the word because all his life people have looked down on him. Called his mum a witch. Sneered at his lifestyle. OK, so he caught a few rabbits but what's wrong with that?'

Ellie sensed from Anna's protectiveness she was still in love with Todd.

'I'm sure the pub staff have told you,' said Anna. 'Owen called Todd a ne'er-do-well. My husband is – was – a purist when it comes to food provenance. He's as concerned about animal welfare as he is staff welfare. Todd wasn't always upfront about where his game came from. I don't know anything about game, or shooting seasons, or any of that, and I'm sure it was all fine, but for Owen, if the paperwork wasn't in place, it was a straight no.' She fiddled with her fingers.

Despite Anna's protestations, it was clear from what Nick had told Ellie that Todd was selling poached game.

'One sweet tea,' said Zoe as she handed a mug to Anna and joined them.

'Thank you. That's so kind.' Anna took a sip. 'Before John took over the pub, and Todd started work there, he kept going in and asking Owen to buy meat. Each time Owen said no. There weren't any arguments but there wasn't any discussion either.'

'That can't have been easy. And what did Todd think of Owen?'

'That he looked down on him and he didn't like that.'

'Did either of them wish the other harm?'

'Not that they mentioned to me.'

'You say you and Todd were planning to get married. How and when were you going to leave Owen?'

'I had already told Owen I wanted a divorce. I wanted a clean break.'

Ellie was thinking about what married life with Todd might have been like for Anna. She was clearly keen to downplay his poaching. To suggest he was, at best, simply trying to feed himself and, at worst, trying to earn enough money to support himself.

Trudy had talked about Todd supplying game on a larger scale, but she might have been misinformed. However, poaching was against the law, and a health risk to the public, and Nick's information had been completely different.

Ellie had known Nick all her life and she trusted him. He wasn't personally involved with Todd like Anna was, and he wasn't someone who bad-mouthed people, unless they'd done wrong and there was a need for the information to be shared.

Ellie recalled Anna saying Owen had been having meetings about finance. She couldn't help wondering where Anna and Todd were planning to live and who was going to pay for the wedding.

'If you don't mind me asking, how were the finances going to work when you left Owen? Were you planning on leaving him with Tollgate Cottage? I ask in case it's relevant to Owen's death.'

'This was the area of contention,' Anna replied. 'Owen had wanted to buy a share in the pub. I wanted us to sell the house so we could split the proceeds.'

'Does that mean you didn't want him to invest in the pub?'

'Correct. I, selfishly, didn't want him to do anything that would delay or complicate the splitting up of our assets. I know that sounds awful but, unfortunately, Todd only had his income from the pub – which was pocket money really – and no capital or assets.'

Sylvia joined the conversation. 'So, were you pleased when John bought the pub on his own?'

Anna's cheeks flushed pink. 'I genuinely didn't know anything about it. It must've been disappointing for Owen and I'm sure he was extremely annoyed about it.'

'But you say you didn't tell him about your affair and plans?'

'No, I didn't mention Todd at all. I simply told him I wanted us to separate.' Anna looked at them through a blur of tears. 'He asked if there was someone else and I denied it. I was trying to be kind.'

Sylvia and Ellie exchanged a knowing look.

'The things I said to you about Owen are true,' Anna added. 'What my sister said to you about us is also true. Owen and I *were* extremely good friends. We did get on well. I just didn't love him anymore, not in a romantic way, and haven't for a while. He knew this. I was honest with him about it. He begged me to stay with him and for a long time that's what I've done.'

It was a mess.

'I know Todd seems a very unlikely choice and probably an unwise one too. But I've loved him since we were teenagers. If it hadn't been for my parents' interference, I wouldn't have married Owen. I'd have married Todd.'

Ellie waited a moment. 'I'm really sorry to ask, but did your husband have a will?'

'Yes. We both did. We were both each other's beneficiaries.'

'Are you sure your husband didn't know anything about your affair?'

'I suppose I can't be certain. But he didn't hear anything about it from me. Or Todd.'

'You don't think Todd might have mentioned it to wind him up?'

'I suppose it's possible, but he said he wouldn't.'

'Apart from you and Todd, who else knew about the affair?'

'Only Gail. She saw us together in the woods, as you know.'

'What happened after that? Did you talk to her about what she'd seen?'

'Unfortunately, there was nothing ambiguous about it so it seemed ridiculous to deny it. I asked her if she was planning on telling Owen, or anyone else, and she said no. That it was our business. She said she knew what it was like to be in an unhappy marriage.'

That was interesting. 'Does that mean she and John aren't happy?'

'We're sisters-in-law but we aren't close. She rarely confides in me, but she's made a few throwaway comments over the years about not sharing John's business ambitions. He wanted a bigger, busier pub and was prepared to make the necessary sacrifices to get it.'

It wasn't a lifestyle that appealed to Ellie at all.

'Such as little time off; unsociable hours,' Anna continued. 'Gail could never persuade John to take a proper holiday as they had to get cover for the pub and he didn't like doing that.'

'Did you trust her when she said she wouldn't tell anyone about Todd?'

'Yes, pretty much.'

'What do you think happened to Owen?'

'I honestly don't know.'

'No hunches or suspicions?'

She shook her head.

'Fears?'

Anna's face contracted. 'That someone had killed him. But nothing about who.'

'In the church CCTV, who do you think the man was in the beige coat and green woolly hat, pushing the wheelbarrow?'

'I haven't a clue. The only thing I can think of is that the restaurant business is ruthless. Owners compete for ratings and awards. Chefs vie for accolades and reviews. Perhaps Owen was involved with something I didn't know about?'

Chapter 35

Sylvia always looked forward to evening bell-ringing practice. She'd been doing it for a couple of months. Kathy from the bakers in the village had suggested it, and Sylvia didn't take much persuading. The sound of the bells always gave her spirits a boost. She loved team activities and this one combined two of her favourite things: chatting and being physically active. What with the spiral staircase at the windmill, her Joe Wicks workouts, and the steep stairs up to the bell tower at the church, Sylvia was sure her glute muscles were stronger than many women her age.

There was, of course, tea and cake too and often the pub afterwards but that wasn't why she went. Well – maybe a bit.

This evening it was Dorothy's turn to supply the 'tea things', as they called them. That meant bring some milk and edibles.

'I made Halloween cupcakes with my granddaughter,' Dorothy said, as she pulled the lid off a Tupperware container. 'They look a bit radioactive,' she said, giggling, 'but they taste delicious. They're orange and chocolate. I've brought a packet of Bourbons and some Jammy Dodgers if anyone doesn't fancy taking the risk.'

'Cora's going to be late,' said Reverend Jackson, who was the Tower Captain. 'So, we'll start without her.'

They were soon ringing.

Sylvia had mastered the basics of managing the rope and controlling the heavy bell above her, and quickly forgot the worries and frustrations of the day. The ringing of the bells, and the physical movements, made her heart open.

Once they'd finished, Dorothy and Sylvia got the tea things ready while the others put out some chairs.

'What's happened to Cora?' Dorothy asked the vicar. 'Did she say?'

'Her son's gone AWOL again and she's very worried,' he replied.

Sylvia knew Cora slightly, not just from bell-ringing, but from the charity shop in the village, where Sylvia volunteered once a week. Cora was a regular, ever on the hunt for bargains.

'Oh dear,' said Dorothy. 'He does give her the run-around, that young man. I've never understood why she didn't cut ties with him when all those people were ill from the meat he sold.'

'What meat?' asked Sylvia.

'The council weren't able to prove it and he denied it, of course,' Dorothy continued. 'And took off, just like he always does when the heat gets too much for him.'

'Poor Cora,' muttered the vicar, his kind features full of sympathy. 'She has a challenging life.'

'*What meat?*' Sylvia asked again, louder this time.

Dorothy drew breath. 'There was a barbecue on the village green here one year. Lots of people went down with food poisoning. Nick Matthews was adamant the meat was poached and came from Todd. When the council tested the burgers, they were made of a mixture of meat, some of which was game which must've been poached, as it wasn't in shooting season.'

'What did Todd say?'

'That they hadn't cooked the burgers long enough.' Dorothy rolled her eyes so exaggeratedly her whole head moved. 'Wouldn't know the truth if it bit him on the bottom, that one.'

Chapter 36

E llie couldn't bear for Anna to be on her own when the two men she loved were dead or missing, so she suggested her friend return to the windmill for another couple of nights' stay.

While Anna was upstairs, soaking in the bath, Ellie and Zoe had nipped out to the local fish and chip shop for some food. Neither of them could put Owen's death out of their mind and, as they waited for their fish to be fried, they continued to discuss possibilities.

'I still cannot get away from what I saw when I went to the window at the windmill,' Ellie whispered. '*Three* people in the balloon basket, reaching up, like they were toasting.'

'I thought we'd agreed, though, Mum. You were mistaken.'

'I know but something doesn't feel right about it.' Ellie scanned her mind for clues. 'Hang on a second. Can I have another look at your picture of the two people in the balloon basket?'

Zoe passed it over.

Ellie squealed. 'That's it, Zo. It *can't* have been Gail and John in the balloon basket together. The two of them are the same height. I noticed when I saw one of their photos, while Gail was unpacking at the pub.' Ellie visualised the image in her mind. Gail had dusted it carefully and Ellie had noticed their height similarity. She'd even commented on it.

They both stared at the image on Zoe's phone, poring over every pixel, willing it to give up its secrets.

'Who was in the basket then?' Zoe re-scrutinised the image. One person was considerably taller than the other.

'Is the taller person a man, do we think?'

'Looks like it, doesn't it?' She stretched the image on her screen, but it quickly became distorted and she returned it to the original size. 'So, was it Gail with a taller man, or John with a smaller woman?'

'There is, of course, a really simple way to find out.' Ellie pursed her lips in concentration. 'We could ask Gail and John. Either of them – or both of them.'

'It's strange, isn't it, because we've already asked Gail and John who went up in the balloon, and they both said *they* did.' Zoe peered over the counter, presumably hoping their food would be ready soon.

'Except we've got proof here that *that* cannot be true,' said Ellie. 'It's not an optical illusion that one person in that basket is much smaller than the other. Their whole frames are different.'

'OK, I know it's unlikely, but could Gail have been sitting down? Is that possible in a balloon basket, do we know?'

'I'm not sure but even if she was sitting down, I still don't think it's the two of them. The build of the two people in this picture is different.' Ellie stared at Zoe. 'I'm going to text Anna, see if she's got a photo of Gail and John together. I've definitely got it stored in my memory that they aren't only the same height; they also have the same physique.'

'Shall I have a look online? See if there are any photos of the two of them at the pub?'

Zoe was quickly on the internet. There were numerous photographs of the new pub owners. John pulling a pint. John outside the pub with a jug of real ale. Gail holding a bouquet of flowers. 'Here we are. Before they bought the place. The two of them behind the bar the day they took over as managers of the Windmill.'

She held the picture out to her mum. 'Same height; similar build. There's no way that was Gail and John in the balloon basket.'

Ellie's words were a whisper: 'Who was it, then?'

Chapter 37
TUESDAY

'Looks like we got here just in time,' Ellie said to Zoe.

In front of them, a giant balloon lay on the grass, semi-inflated, the basket on its side. Behind it, the sunrise stretched across the sky – a band of red, yellow and gold.

Ellie recognised James Gould from Nick's description: baseball cap, thick red hair, chunky build. She waved.

'Morning.' He gave them a grin. 'Still time for you to join us, if you'd like to. See what it's all about. You might get the bug, you never know.'

Ellie's stomach somersaulted. 'That's very kind, thank you. I won't though.'

James stepped away from the canvas and the basket, and joined Ellie and Zoe. 'I gather you've got some questions relating to the chef who went missing.'

'That's right.' Ellie explained the scenario.

'Correct me if I've got it wrong. When you saw the balloon, you thought there were three people in the basket, and when your daughter saw it, there were two, and the balloon was rising.'

'That's right,' said Ellie.

'I'm sure you've already considered that one or both of you may have misperceived what was there. Eyesight limitations. Fatigue. Sleepiness. Light in your eyes. Shadows. Any number of things...'

'We have.'

'And I'm presuming the balloon didn't land, let a passenger out, take off a second time and land again?'

'Not that the pilot and his party told us.'

'It would certainly have been more complicated. A simpler explanation is that in between *you* seeing the balloon,' he looked at Ellie, 'and your daughter, one of the passengers ... er ... left the basket.' He stopped there and raised his eyebrows slightly. 'Given Zoe said the balloon was rising, I suspect this option is most likely.'

'Ah. Why's that?' Ellie felt the glimmers of excitement. Were they finally about to find out what happened?

'Change of weight in the basket affects the equilibrium. If you have three passengers and their average weight is, say, twelve stone. If twelve stone suddenly leaves the basket of a hot air balloon, it will shoot up in the air until it regains equilibrium.'

'You mean someone fell out or was pushed out.'

'Precisely.'

Ellie glanced at Zoe. 'Thank you. That's very helpful.'

'Probably not what you want to hear when somebody who was due to go on a hot air balloon ride goes missing, but ...'

'No, but we've given our word to his wife that we'll discover the truth.'

Zoe spoke now. 'We're also wondering about where it's claimed the balloon took off. The pilot, his wife and the person who was crewing for them say they inflated and launched the balloon in the field on the coast side of Hawking Down. At the bottom, near the road.'

'And you want to know whether I believe them?'

'Yes.'

'I think it's highly unlikely. I flew on Saturday morning and the wind was westerly, so it would have blown them straight across the road and over the sea. An experienced pilot would know that and would therefore have chosen a launch site that wasn't so close to both hazards.'

James paused and seemed to be thinking. 'I know the spot. Yes, there's parking there. And it's ideal when you have an easterly wind. However, I gather we're talking about a take-off of 7am.'

Ellie nodded.

'They're more likely to have used a location where they could drive straight onto the field, unload, inflate the balloon and take off safely.' He pointed at his own balloon. 'We specifically chose this site for this morning because the wind is easterly, and we don't want to be blown onto the power lines.'

They heard someone calling.

James gave his crew a thumbs-up. 'I'm going to have to go, I'm afraid. We're almost ready for take-off. If you've got any more questions, or you'd like anything elaborated, give me a ring on the mobile. Happy to help.' He raised his hand in a parting gesture. 'By the way – the obvious place to launch the balloon on Saturday morning would have been the top of Hawking Down.'

Chapter 38

Sylvia preferred it when the shop was busy, as the time passed more quickly and her back ached less. She had a feeling today was going to be one such day.

Since she'd started work at 8.30am, there'd been a steady stream of customers, scouring the shelves for charity bargains and much-needed items. She'd already sold a tall flower vase to a young mum; two towels to a dog-owner; an egg cup to a student, and a leather handbag to Helen from the hairdresser's.

She'd also put out two boxes of books. Although she sometimes felt a bit mean about it, the manager said it was fine for the volunteers to have first dibs on anything they fancied. Despite the fact she'd been married to a detective, Sylvia was partial to crime fiction, and she'd snatched up the first in a new series set around Dover and the castle. She'd even managed to skim the first couple of pages while

Gladys Blackman tried on welly boots in the changing room.

'What do you think of these?' Gladys asked, sashaying across the carpet in a pair of green boots with a large sunflower on each side. This was the fourth pair she'd taken a fancy to.

'Very pretty, but I think they're children's. If you like them, I'm sure it doesn't matter as long as they fit you.'

'It's one benefit of being a size four.' Gladys grinned, pleased as Punch. 'I'll take them. There's even room for an extra pair of socks. They'll be perfect for the fireworks display. Are you going?'

'Yes. We'll all be there.'

On the radio in the stockroom, the news was on low. The manager was in there sorting through clothes deliveries. 'Awful about that young man washing up on the beach, isn't it? Can't imagine what his family must be going through.'

Gladys perked up at the potential for some gossip.

'I wonder how long it will take for the police to identify him?' the manager continued.

'And then there's the other one,' added Gladys, 'who turned up in the churchyard.'

'I'm sure we'll hear soon,' said Sylvia. 'The main thing – for the families – is finding out what happened and being able to bury them.'

'My grandson was in the woods with a friend on Friday evening,' said Gladys. 'They jog, or whatever it's called.'

'"Run", I think is the term,' Sylvia said.

Gladys shrugged. 'Anyway – he said he heard shots. At first, he wasn't sure whether it was fireworks. Then he wondered if it was a car backfiring, but Jason said he was sure it was a shotgun.'

'Which woods?' Sylvia and the manager chorused.

'Appledown. Behind the garden centre.'

'Really?' Sylvia was eager to learn more. 'Ellie and Zoe thought they heard shots when they were walking home from the Rattling Cat on Friday night.'

'I didn't say anything to Jason, but it made me wonder if that poacher chap is back, shooting deer and flogging it.'

Sylvia's ears pricked up. 'Do you mean Todd Reynolds?'

The manager, who was listening to their conversation and interjecting at intervals, poked her head around the door.

'That's him,' said Gladys, scowling. 'One year at Christmas, he was going round houses in the village. Sold me and a few others some venison, and we found out it was from a hind.'

'No? It's illegal to shoot the females at that time of year.' Animal cruelty incensed Sylvia.

'My son was furious,' Gladys continued. 'Installed one of those video doorbell things the next day so we had evidence if he did it again.'

'And did he?'

'Thankfully, no. But I'll tell you this for nothing. He's from a family of wrong-uns, he is. Mother's a witch and–'

'Wait a minute,' said Sylvia. 'Reynolds? Is his father Vincent Reynolds, from Sandwich? The second-hand car dealer.'

'That's him,' said Gladys firmly, pulling her chin in. 'Car dealer, my eye. Burglar, more like. From what I've heard, the apples don't fall far from *that* tree.'

'That's interesting. I used to work with Vincent's social worker. Never had the, er ... *pleasure* of meeting Vincent himself though. Well, well.' Sylvia waved at the manager and then turned to Gladys. 'Excuse me a minute. I need to make an urgent phone call.'

She strode into the back of the shop and fished her phone out of her bag.

Chapter 39

Having watched James Gould's balloon take off, Ellie and Zoe collected Finn, Rebus and Agatha from the windmill and went straight to Hawking Down. The temperature had risen a fraction, but Ellie was still glad of the warmth from her scarf and coat. The sky had shifted from a rather lovely blue to a brooding white with pink-y-grey wisps.

The grass was thin and spiky. The dogs chased each other merrily, sniffing out smells and relishing the open space.

A rabbit appeared. Then another, and a third. Rebus and Agatha launched themselves into the air with frenzied yelps and hurtled after the unsuspecting creatures. But the dogs were too slow, thankfully, and all the noise had alerted the rabbits, giving them enough time to escape into the bushes and into their warrens.

'If John and Gail drove up this way,' said Finn, 'there are several spots where they could have taken the balloon straight onto the grass for inflation.'

'It's quite wet so, with any luck, there might be tyre marks,' said Ellie. 'There can't be that many people round here who want to launch a hot air balloon–'

'*And* have a pilot's licence,' Zoe added.

'Exactly,' said Finn. 'And there wouldn't be any other reason to bring a vehicle onto the grass. Let's split up and walk along the edge of the field where it joins the car park, shall we?' He bent over to examine the ground. 'According to John, the three of them inflated the balloon so that's three sets of footprints we're looking for, *and* tyre marks.'

'John had a Land Rover parked on the drive at his place when we were there,' said Zoe. She swiped her phone screen and tapped. 'The tyres will vary by model and brand. Yes, here's one.' She showed them both the image she'd just found. 'A wide tyre and a specific tread.'

As they walked, Finn threw sticks at intervals for Rebus and Agatha. Most of the time they both went after the same one and then had a tug of war over it.

'Here we are, look,' said Zoe. 'Tyre marks going from the car park onto the field.'

Finn joined her and they followed the marks to the point where they stopped.

'James had his balloon tethered to the bars on the front of his vehicle this morning,' said Zoe. 'So, let's walk forwards from here, side by side.'

'What are we looking for?' Ellie asked.

'I don't really know. Signs of something going wrong. A struggle perhaps?'

They walked ahead, eyes pinned to the area at their feet. Very quickly they came to a patch of ground with shards of glass scattered in the radius of a metre or so.

'Hang on. I recognise this.' Zoe picked up a piece of the distinctive green glass with white enamel on it. 'It's from a champagne bottle. Why would it be shattered?'

'Perhaps they dropped it,' Ellie suggested.

'Neither Gail nor John mentioned dropping the fizz though,' said Zoe. 'I suppose they might not have thought it was important but it's not exactly cheap.'

'Maybe there was a fight?' Ellie turned to face them. 'I very much doubt it's a coincidence they didn't mention smashing the champagne bottle. More likely they omitted it because they didn't want us to know. Why might that be?' She crouched down and took a few pictures on her phone. 'There's definitely been a scuffle here. The grass has got chunks out of it where someone has moved at an angle and landed heavily.'

Zoe crouched next to her. 'And here, someone's pulled the grass out, like they were dragging themselves along – or *being* dragged.'

Ellie bagged up a couple of bits of glass with one of Rebus' poo bags. 'There's no doubt a bottle was broken here. You know, I'm starting to wonder – if John and Gail lied about this, what else might they not have told the truth about?'

Chapter 40

On the way back from Hawking Down, Ellie suggested stopping off at McDonald's to ask if any of the staff had seen Owen drop his car off. As they pulled into the car park, she spotted a staff member sitting on the kerb, over a hundred metres from the building, smoking a cigarette.

Zoe and Finn stayed in the car while Ellie went in. It was busier than when she and Sylvia were here, but it was hardly thriving. She scoured the scene for Ryan, the manager she'd spoken to last time. But no luck, so she approached a till. 'Could I speak to your manager, please? It's about the man who–'

'Sure. I'll get her for you.' The girl rang a bell and a flashing red light lit up at the top of her till.

A young woman appeared. Grey uniform, purple hair and a smiley face.

'Lady for you,' the cashier said, pointing at Ellie.

'I'm Miranda. How can I help?'

Ellie introduced herself. She got out her phone, showed her Owen's photograph, and explained the situation. 'So, did you or any of your staff see this man park his car in the spaces by the hawthorn bushes and the flower bed, at around 6am on Saturday morning?'

'I wasn't working that day,' Miranda replied, 'but I can ask around.'

Ellie remembered the person she'd seen smoking when they arrived. 'Your staff who smoke–'

'We don't encourage it.'

'No, I meant, they might have seen Owen park his car. They're right by where he left it.'

'I'll see what I can do,' said Miranda, but her tone hardly filled Ellie with hope.

Ellie decided to go for the sympathy vote. 'It's just, he went missing... and now, unfortunately, he's dead.'

—ele—

Five minutes later, on the way home, Ellie's phone rang.

She pressed 'answer' on the Bluetooth system.

'Hi. Is that Mrs Blix?'

'It is.'

'It's Miranda here, from McDonald's. You're in luck. Two of our probationers were having a cigarette break in the car park when your friend's vehicle was left.'

'You're kidding?' screeched Zoe, right in Ellie's ear.

'Thank you. Excuse my daughter. And it was definitely Owen who parked the car?'

'That's the thing. No, it wasn't. It wasn't him at all. And it wasn't as early as you were suggesting.'

As Miranda told them what the probationers had seen, Ellie realised that this was the missing piece they'd been looking for; the one that completed the jigsaw.

'That's it,' Ellie told Zoe. 'I've figured it out. I know who killed Owen and Todd. And I suspect they have another person in their sights who knows too much.'

'What?' It was another screech. 'In that case, we've got to stop them before they kill someone else.'

Chapter 41

Finn and Zoe ushered the people Ellie wanted present into the function room at the Windmill Inn. At least with the killer in the room, there should be no more deaths. Dave was on his way and could take over once she'd identified the culprit. That was what they'd always done before.

Sylvia arrived, puffing. 'Sorry. Dashed here from the shop.' She took off her coat and beret. Ellie had rung and updated her on who their culprits were and what the evidence was.

Ellie glanced around the room. The vicar had an avuncular arm round Anna's tiny shoulders. Trudy was next to Anna, her expression full of anguish. John and Gail were by the fireplace. Gail was chewing her cheek anxiously. John was adding logs to the fire, as though they were settling in for an afternoon's entertainment. George was standing as far away from the Fields as he could. Todd's mother sat at a table, cheeks and neck flecked pink.

Ellie took a swig of water from a bottle. 'This case was a paradox from the start, but then, murders so often are. When people are killed, we regularly find things aren't how they seem, because killers go to great lengths to conceal their crimes. And this couldn't have been truer here.'

She glanced at Sylvia, who gave her an encouraging nod. 'It started with me seeing three people in a hot air balloon basket and Zoe seeing the same balloon a short time later with two people in it. There was only ever going to be a few explanation combinations but my, we've been round the houses, haven't we?'

Sylvia joined Ellie at her side. 'There have been a number of theories about what might have happened to Owen. Anna, you were convinced he'd had an accident. John and Gail, you thought he'd blown you out to go to a business meeting.'

There was a loud knock on a window. It was Dave.

Finn let him in.

Ellie turned to John. 'Perhaps we can start with the balloon flight. Would you like to talk us through it?'

John brushed log dust off his hands and cleared his throat. 'Sure. When Owen cancelled, Gail and I thought nothing of it, so, although we were disappointed, we decided to proceed with the flight. It was our anniversary, and all the kit was loaded in the Land Rover. George had agreed to crew before take-off and on landing. He and I started inflating the balloon, with Gail's help. When the time was right, Gail and I got in the basket, didn't we darling?'

He looked over at Gail, who gave a curt nod.

John continued. 'George stood by the balloon basket, leaning on the edge, as is customary, holding it down while I carried on heating the balloon for take-off. When the balloon was ready, George let go of the basket and off we went, landing about half an hour later.' He looked round proudly. 'A shorter trip than we'd planned but there we are.'

'Thank you,' said Ellie, keeping her gaze on him. 'Except that isn't what happened, is it?'

The room went quiet. All eyes were on her.

'Er ... what d'you mean?' said John.

Ellie turned to Gail. 'You told me Owen texted John, saying he wasn't coming on the balloon ride.'

'I made a mistake,' she countered quickly.

'It wasn't though, was it? If they haven't already – when the police check your husband's phone records, and Owen's, do you think they'll find the text message from Owen?'

She stared at Ellie, blinking.

The room was quiet, everyone rapt.

'It's a fair question, isn't it?'

'I assume they will,' Gail replied.

'Or – will they find a call from Owen to your husband in both of their phone records?'

'I don't know. I ... I'm not technical.'

'Or neither, perhaps?'

Gail frowned. 'What d'you mean?'

'I feel sorry for you, Gail. I'm sure you didn't want any of this. But it's happened. And two men are dead.' She turned back to John. 'It wasn't George who helped with inflating the balloon, was it? *Or* who met you on landing?'

He scowled at her. 'Yes, it was. How else would we have got the balloon home?' He cast about, smiling, as though he hoped his comment proved Ellie wrong.

Gail's expression was twitchy and nervous.

'Oh, I'm sure you had help. What I mean is; it wasn't from George. Was it?'

She looked now at John's barman. 'Could you confirm for us, please, that you met a fellow runner at Deal Pier at 6am on Saturday morning?'

George stared at the floor, nodding.

'Chap called Will Lodge. Arranged through Wootton Runners on Facebook.' Ellie held up her phone showing the screenshot. 'Zoe's printed it out for the police.'

'Yes,' mumbled George.

'So, you did *not* in fact crew for your employers either before or after their hot air balloon flight, despite saying you did?'

'Er ...' He shuffled from one foot to the other. 'Um ...'

'Did you or didn't you?'

'I did not,' he replied, blushing profusely. 'We've got a baby on the way and our rent's shot up. Claire's lost her job and John paid me to say I crewed for him.' He was staring at the ground. 'I didn't know anything about Owen having come to harm. John said it was just so he didn't get into trouble for not having any crew.'

Ellie took a deep breath. 'Thank you. We'll leave the police to deal with that.'

She turned back to John. His narrowed eyes suggested the information had sunk in. 'So, who crewed for you?' Ellie hurled the question at him.

John exchanged a look with his wife and didn't answer.

'Do you want to tell us?' said Ellie. 'If not, I can give everyone the information.'

'You're bluffing,' he growled.

'Shall we test that? The person who crewed for you was–'

'OK, OK. We were going to do it between the three of us,' John replied. 'Owen, Gail and myself. Leave Owen's car over Kingsdown way as that was where the wind was going to blow us.'

Ellie let him talk. She was keen to hear his explanation.

'But because Owen didn't turn up, that wasn't possible. We landed the balloon, deflated it, and I called a cab to take Gail back to get the Land Rover while I stayed with the balloon. She then came back and picked me up.'

Ellie caught the frown on Gail's face.

'You called a cab to marshland in the middle of nowhere?'

'There's a track.'

'Which cab company?'

'I can't remember.'

'But it'll be in your phone records, right?'

He shrugged.

'Perhaps you can't remember because that wasn't what happened. You see, we know who crewed for you. But I'll come back to that in a minute. The thing is, far more importantly, I don't think *you* went in that balloon basket at all on Saturday.'

John muttered under his breath. 'How'd you work that out?'

'It's bugged me ever since that morning. I thought I saw three people in the basket but couldn't be certain because the sun was shining in my eyes, and I'd only just woken up. But Zoe *was* certain. Weren't you?' She stretched her hand out to Zoe, indicating for her to take over.

'Yup.' Zoe surveyed the room. 'And – I took a photo on my phone which clearly shows *two people*.'

John rolled his eyes. 'Yes – my wife and me.'

'We'll come back to exactly *who* went up in the balloon. The thing is, the photo, which we've printed out for the police, shows two people of very different sizes, both in terms of height and build.' She pointed at Finn, who was holding a pile of print-outs for Dave. 'Do pass it round. I've got the original on my phone.'

Finn handed it to Anna.

'It was taken by me from my bedroom at the windmill, and although I took the photo from a lot lower than the balloon's height,' she pointed upwards, 'the angle would have been the same for both passengers in the basket.'

'Is there a point here?' said John.

'There certainly is,' Zoe replied. 'You see, it cannot have been a trick of perception that the two people looked different.'

She walked over to Gail, who was standing next to John, and gestured to their heights. 'I think we can all agree that they have similar heights and physiques, yes?'

Everyone nodded.

'And given the photo shows two people of very different heights, I think we can also all agree it *cannot* have been John and Gail in the balloon basket, as they claim. Yes?' She looked from Gail to John. 'Would one of you like to explain who went up in the balloon?' She fixed her gaze on John. 'Two people or three? And who were they?'

Gail's head was lowered. John stared at Zoe, eyes blazing.

'Was it Gail and someone else, or John and someone else? Or were there three people all along? You see, Mum initially assumed she'd made a mistake. Trick of the light or tired eyes. That sort of thing. But Finn found a witness who *also* saw three people in the balloon basket. That suggests Mum *wasn't* imagining things.' She stared straight at John. 'Who were those three people?'

'For the last time,' he replied with a sigh, 'there were two people in the balloon, and they were my wife and me. It was our wedding anniversary. We had a short ride, breakfast in the air and then I went to work.'

'Lovely,' said Zoe, changing tack. 'Champagne breakfast, was it?'

John frowned, presumably having expected Zoe to continue with her previous line. 'As a matter of fact, it was. But we had no idea at that point that something had happened to Owen.'

'I love champagne. Don't you?' She twiddled with her plait. 'What brand was it?'

John stared at her as though she was a bit loopy. 'Er … my wife got it.' He shot a hopeful glance at Gail.

Zoe stepped forward and turned to Gail. 'Could you help?' She was scrolling on her phone. 'Was it … Moet & Chandon, Bollinger, Perrier Jouet, Veuve Clicquot?'

'Er, Moet, I think.'

'Are you sure?'

'What d'you mean?'

'Finn and I searched where the balloon took off on top of Hawking Down.'

'That was *not* where we launched,' said John. 'It was in the field the road side of the down.'

Zoe shook her head. 'That's what you've wanted us to believe. But it's not what the evidence points at. We found tyre marks on top of Hawking Down which look like they're from a Land Rover. The police will no doubt be able to confirm if that's true and if they're from yours.'

She flashed a look at Dave who gave her a proud smile. 'We also found some glass there. Pretty, decorated glass…'

John spoke up. 'This is all very nice but–'

'Now, I used to work behind the bar here at the Windmill Inn,' Zoe said, cutting him off, 'and we sold lots of champagne. I recognised the glass we found. This is the bottle it's from.' She showed Gail a photograph on her phone. 'And this is a snap of one of the pieces of glass we found on Hawking Down, near the Land Rover tyre marks.' She showed her the phone again. 'They look identical, don't they?'

Gail nodded.

'Could you read out the label?'

'Perrier Jouët Belle Époque 2012.'

'And was that the brand you bought for your anniversary balloon ride?'

She nodded.

'There's another reason I recognised the glass. I passed my driving test recently and Dad bought me a bottle of Perrier Jouët Belle Époque. It's got pretty white flowers on green glass. I looked up their history. They're Japanese white anemones, created by Emile Galle in 1902.'

'Well, it must be a coincidence,' John stated gruffly. 'We definitely took our bottle up in the balloon with us. Perrier Jouët is a popular brand. I sell dozens of bottles a week in the pub and–'

Zoe wagged her finger at him. 'I don't think you did. In fact, I think the broken glass we found is from *your* bottle. And – judging by the scuffed ground nearby – I suspect there was a struggle or fight of some sort, involving the champagne bottle. I'm right, aren't I?'

'No. You're completely deluded. This is pure fiction.' He looked pointedly at Dave. 'Are you going to allow this?'

'Absolutely.' Dave folded his arms over his chest. 'She's doing a great job.'

Ellie was pleased John's attempts at intimidation weren't working. Outwardly, anyway. She was itching to jump in and help Zoe, but she stopped herself. Zoe had been determined she wanted to cover this stage, and she had the information to pull it off.

'Did you lie about where the balloon took off from so that no-one would find the broken glass?'

John frowned.

'You see, we spoke to a hot air balloon expert, and he told us there's no way an experienced balloonist like yourself would've used the spot you claimed, because you'd have been blown straight over the road into the sea.'

John's eyes narrowed.

'He went even further than that, suggesting where was more likely. And hey presto, it didn't take long to find your broken champagne bottle.'

John grunted.

Gail was frozen to the spot.

Zoe walked towards John, Finn alongside her now. 'Would you mind removing your hat for a moment?'

'Why?'

'I'd like to check something.' She placed her hands on his arms and guided him to turn round so that the back of his head was facing the room.

Begrudgingly, John pulled his cap off, revealing dark scabs in hair that was matted with blood in places.

'Thank you. Mum noticed your injuries in the pub kitchen on Sunday.'

'Like I said, I bashed my head in the cellar.'

'I'm sure the police will be able to test the cuts for glass fragments. We suspect it wasn't a work injury at all. Isn't it true that someone took a swing at you with the champagne bottle?'

'No. It is not.'

Zoe ignored him. 'The question is: who?' She drummed her fingers on her chin.

Sylvia gave Zoe a proud smile and took over. 'We don't think your brother went to McDonald's at all. We think he arrived for the balloon ride as planned with you and Gail. And he might've felt like bashing you over the head with a glass bottle after you bought the pub from under him, but we don't think it was Owen.'

'No way. I've told you. He cancelled. We didn't see him. Gail, tell them.'

Gail was studying her hands, pulling at the skin round her nails.

Sylvia carried on. 'And it's true, isn't it, that he was in the balloon basket with Gail? So, let's return to the question of who crewed for you. That'll clarify things. We're back to the question of, if it wasn't George, who was it?'

John had replaced his cap and gone to stand next to Gail, his arm round her shoulders. She was as stiff as an ironing board in his grip.

'Finn's got two screenshots from the CCTV from Saturday evening at St Mary's church. The first one shows a man pushing another man in a wheelbarrow over to a tomb in the graveyard.'

She paused while everyone took in what she'd just told them, and while Finn handed out prints of the video. 'I realise this isn't a sight we see in Lower Wootton often, thankfully; a dead man being pushed in a wheelbarrow.'

There were gasps around the room.

Sylvia continued: 'In the next image, another man helps open the tomb and put the dead man in.'

'Appalling behaviour,' chuntered Reverend Jackson.

'We know from Anna's appeal on the village's Facebook page, on Saturday morning, that Owen was wearing a navy jacket, black jeans, blue Nike trainers and a red jumper when he left home, so this strongly suggests the dead man is Owen.'

Anna gasped and reached out for support.

'How did you describe Todd Reynolds to us?' she asked Anna, who blushed.

'The height of a baseball player,' she said, softly, 'and the build of a scaffolder.'

'We've cropped your husband out of this picture so it's safe for you to look at.' Sylvia showed her the image. 'Could you tell us if you think this man could be Todd?'

She gasped and nodded, pointing at the tattoo on Todd's face, which Zoe had enlarged. 'He had a teardrop tattoo just here.' She touched her left cheek, the soft part just below her eye, as though she was imagining Todd in front of her and touching his skin.

'Thank you.' Sylvia turned back to John. 'I put it to you, Mr Field, that the third man in this still from the CCTV, helping Todd Reynolds to bury your brother, is … *you*.'

'Absolute rubbish.'

'And given the three of you were together in the grave-yard, it's our belief that Owen joined you on Hawking Down for the balloon ride–'

'No. No. No.' John's face was like thunder.

Alarm streaked Gail's features.

'Todd Reynolds crewed for you, didn't he? He's a long-standing contact of yours from Canterbury who's been supplying game to your pubs for several years.'

'No.'

'You lied about it being him, and paid your barman to lie for you, because you knew you were going to have to dispose of Todd.'

'Unless you have some solid evidence, I would advise you to be careful about what you're saying.' John made his voice deliberately intimidating.

Dave sucked in a breath and shifted on the spot.

This was exactly what they'd expected John to say.

Ellie took over now. 'D'you think we'd gather everyone here if we didn't have evidence? No, of course you don't. It's *you* who's bluffing.' She paused briefly. 'Let's go back to the beginning. To the hot air balloon and *Todd's* murder.'

Anna gasped.

Ellie faced her.

'Todd was angry when you broke things off with him, wasn't he?'

Anna nodded.

'Would you describe him as very angry?'

'Extremely.'

'And who did he blame?'

'Owen. Although it wasn't Owen's fault.'

'Could you explain that?'

'I was going to leave Owen and get divorced so Todd and I could get married and go travelling together.'

'In a campervan? We saw the brochures beside your bed.'

'Yes. But I couldn't go through with it.' She shook her head, eyes closed, as if what she had been contemplating really was unimaginable. 'Owen has always been a decent man and I felt terrible about hurting him. So, I broke things off with Todd. Todd blamed Owen. He saw Owen as the impediment to our eventual marriage.'

'An angler has told us Todd bought some fish off him around 5am on Saturday and carelessly mentioned he was off to crew for a hot air balloon ride on Hawking Down.'

'What angler?' John snarled. 'You're making this up.'

'I can assure you I'm not,' Ellie replied. 'We've spoken to him ourselves and verified his account. And we found Todd's battered old bicycle in the undergrowth on the bank at Hawking Down, amongst some rubbish. Did you chuck it there after you murdered him?'

'Absolutely not.'

'Perhaps when Todd agreed to crew for you, he didn't have violence in mind. But it clearly triggered him when Anna broke up with him, and perhaps seeing Owen provoked him further.'

'It's all my fault,' said Anna through tears. 'I had no idea Todd was crewing for the balloon ride.'

'Isn't it true that Todd swung at you with the champagne bottle, giving you those cuts?'

'No.' John was shaking his head, trying to laugh and pretend it was all a joke, or a drama.

'Did that blow knock you out?'

'I've told you. I banged my head on a beam in the cellar at the pub.'

'I'm not buying that, I'm afraid.' Ellie spun round to Gail. 'Did Todd knock your husband out with the champagne bottle and jump into the balloon basket after that?'

'Er ...' A look of panic spread over her face. 'John?'

'We know Todd flew with you and your husband frequently, and although he wasn't qualified to do so, he knew how to fire up the burner. Is that what he did? And the balloon took off.'

'No,' boomed John.

'If you were knocked out, you won't be able to answer.' She turned from John to Gail. 'Did Owen see Todd hit your husband and jump into the basket? Then tackled Todd?'

'Don't answer her,' shouted John.

'Gail?'

'I ...'

'What I *thought* was three people raising glasses in a toast was actually a struggle in the basket. Wasn't it? Did Todd pull a knife? Or was there a struggle to switch the burner off, to get the balloon to land before it got too high? And Todd bundled Owen out of the basket, and he fell to his death?'

'This is pure fiction,' John insisted.

'You would say that, wouldn't you? Except it's actually more sinister than Todd bundling your brother out of the balloon basket in a fit of jealous rage.' Ellie paused. 'What I'm wondering about is what Todd had on *you* and your wife, for you to collude with covering up your brother's death.'

'I'm not listening to this.'

'I think you'll want to. You see, someone in the village told me all about Todd Reynolds' nefarious activities over the years. And how you and Todd set up a supplier selling Todd's poached game until, in the face of complaints and opposition, you jacked it in. I suspect you've been up to your neck buying illegal game from Todd for years. And he threatened to expose you if you handed him into the police ... I'm right, aren't I?'

'Owen was not there. Nor was Todd. It was Gail and–'

'Were you involved with the supply of barbecue meat that caused food poisoning? Did you help Todd to make the whole thing go away? It won't be hard for the police to check.'

'I don't know anything about that.'

'OK. Let's try a different tack. Let's go back to the hot air balloon expert Zoe spoke to.' Ellie signalled to Zoe to take over again.

'Yes,' Zoe said. 'He told me that when a balloon rises sharply, one reason can be because a weight has left the basket.'

Ellie peered at John, watching for the penny to drop.

'For example, if a passenger fell out,' Zoe continued. 'Or ... was *pushed* out.'

The atmosphere in the room changed immediately.

John pulled himself up straight, his face muscles twitching.

Ellie resumed. 'From the start, you were keen to tell us your brother had gone to meet someone. How he'd been having business meetings at odd hours–'

'He had been.'

'... and that he'd left his car at McDonald's.'

'He did.'

'Yet the staff there – who recognise him *and* you – didn't see him on Saturday morning.'

'Temporary staff, probably.'

'No. The manager has worked there for a year, and he says your brother *definitely* wasn't in the store. And before you say he probably forgot or wasn't looking properly, he very kindly checked the CCTV for us.' She looked over at Dave. 'And has kept it for the police.'

'Then there was the Dear John letter you wrote Anna – using Owen's favourite nylon-tipped pen – hoping to convince her that Owen had gone to crew on a yacht in the south of France. Handily, your handwriting has always been very similar to his.'

John flinched.

'But hardly consistent with a man who leaves her love notes around the house. A graphologist will quickly verify that.' Ellie took another swig of water. 'Back to McDonald's now. You see, a staff member saw you, parking Owen's car and leaving it there.'

'Impossible.'

'It's not. He was having a cigarette near where you parked because the manager doesn't like the staff smoking right outside the restaurant. He recognised you because he's seen you before, getting food late at night. He also said your head was bleeding and you were holding a tissue to it.'

John tutted contemptuously.

'There's something else. When you said you checked whether Owen had gone to McDonald's, we believed you. But you didn't, did you? It didn't occur to me to confirm with the manager when we first went in. But as soon as we learnt you'd dropped your brother's car off there, I did.'

John muttered.

'The manager was as adamant about you *not* going into the branch as he was about your brother also not going there.' Ellie glanced round the room. This next bit was going to clinch it. 'That got me wondering. Why might you not check whether he'd been there?'

'You tell me. You seem to have all the answers.'

'The obvious answer is if you *knew* all along he hadn't.' She waited for the sentence to sink in. 'And if you knew exactly what had happened to him. Because you do, don't you? Both of you.' She looked from John to Gail and back again.

'That's quite an accusation,' said John.

'Fortunately, we have proof. And time is up. You invented the whole McDonald's story to deflect attention from you and your wife. I'm right, aren't I?'

'Absolute twaddle.'

'Shall we go through the balloon ride again? Gail, you're the only person who can testify to what actually happened, as your husband was out cold.'

'It's no good, John. The truth's going to come out.' Gail's face was defiant and determined. 'When all those people got sick from the meat you sold the barbecue organisers, I told you I'd had enough. I'm not lying for you anymore.' She turned to Ellie. 'Todd, John and Owen inflated the balloon.'

John's face was apoplectic. 'Don't do this. They're bluffing.'

'No,' she said, her voice much more confident now. 'That's it. You're on your own. I want a divorce. I've gone along with your schemes for years and I can't do it a moment longer.'

John lunged for the door.

Dave got there first and blocked his way. 'Let's hear what she's got to say, shall we?' he said.

Gail cleared her throat. 'We were almost ready to take off. I was in the balloon basket with John and Owen. John got out to go back to the car to get the champagne, which he'd left in the boot in the cold bag. I've flown with John numerous times, and I continued to heat the balloon. Todd was standing by the basket, leaning on the edge, holding it down.'

'Then what?' asked Ellie.

'As John approached the basket, Todd said, "Shall I take that while you get in?", meaning the champagne. John handed it to him, and Todd swung it at John, smashing it on the back of John's head, knocking him over. I was stunned and terrified. Todd has extraordinary strength and is very agile. Comes from years of living in the woods, and hunting, I think. He vaulted into the basket and turned the burner up full, and the balloon took off.'

'With him, you and Owen in it?' asked Ellie.

'Yes. Owen tried to tackle him but was quickly over-powered. Owen was no wimp, but Todd was in a league of his own. There was a scuffle over a knife.'

'A knife?'

'Yes, Todd always carried a knife. He used it for ...' Her sentence petered out.

'Poaching,' stated Ellie.

'Yes. Within what seemed like a few minutes, Todd had lifted Owen up by his legs and shoved him out of the basket.' She closed her eyes. 'The scream. It was ...'

She reached out for a chair to steady herself. 'I told Todd we needed to land as quickly as possible, but I was scared to be too forceful about it in case he decided to tip me out too.'

Must've been terrifying for Gail, thought Ellie.

'Luckily, by the time we touched down, John had come round and managed to follow us in the Land Rover.'

'We have you on CCTV, Mr Field, helping Todd dispose of your brother's body,' said Ellie, 'so I'm assuming you and Todd fetched Owen's body, waited 'til it was dark and then disposed of it in the tomb?'

John sighed.

'Given you transported his body in your vehicle, there's likely to be trace evidence in it: fibres, hair, blood, saliva. Plenty for the police to analyse, in case you think you'll deny your way out of it.'

He closed his eyes.

'We now need to discuss Todd's murder. We know he'd been supplying you with poached game for years at your old pub in Canterbury.'

'Not true.'

'Having disposed of your brother's body with him, I would imagine you then couldn't risk him remaining alive.'

'Also untrue.'

'We have a witness, we'll call him "G". He saw Todd placing the gnome on the pier before he, Todd, met you. This same witness was so curious about what Todd was up to, he followed him along the pier to the bar there. And it's how most murderers are caught in the end. They slip up. You weren't very careful, were you? Who do you think the witness saw, meeting Todd?'

John shrugged.

'*You*. G didn't suspect anything and didn't follow you. What do you think the pier CCTV will show when the police check it?'

He shrugged.

'For example, will it show you murdering Todd and pushing his body off the pier into the sea?'

'Oh, for goodness' sake, John,' shouted Gail. 'Tell the truth, for once in your life. Todd had been a liability for years and had got worse.'

John exhaled deeply. He flopped down onto a bar stool, head in hands, all bravado extinguished. 'Todd wanted money to start a new life with Anna and he started blackmailing me. Saying he'd tell the authorities about the game I'd bought from him for years in Canterbury and since taking over the pub here in Wootton.'

'Game that was poached.'

'Some of it was, yes.'

'Most of it was,' snarled Gail. 'Todd told us if he went down for Owen's murder, he'd take us with him.'

Anna gasped.

'Made it clear he'd say it was *us* who killed Owen, and it would be our word against his.'

A sob rang out in the room. Anna was hanging onto the vicar's arm.

'Everyone talked about Todd as if he was ...' Gail gave Cora an apologetic look, 'a bit dim. But he wasn't. He was extremely sharp and very dangerous.'

Ellie recalled Gail's comments about Todd's unsuitability.

'He'd recorded a lot of his conversations with John,' Gail continued, 'so that, whenever he got into hot water, he could blackmail John into covering for him.'

Ellie fixed her gaze on John. 'So, you arranged to meet him on the pier and stabbed him with his own poaching knife. Then shoved him in the sea.'

'Tell the truth,' Gail screamed. 'Just tell the damn truth.'

'The bar at the end of the pier has CCTV all round it,' said Ellie. 'It won't take the police long to find it.'

John's face was tight with fury.

'We also found Todd's rucksack in the undergrowth at Hawking Down. It'll have your prints on it.'

Finally, John nodded, his gaze lowered now. 'Anna, I'm sorry. I know you loved them both.' He swallowed. 'I wouldn't have killed Todd if he hadn't killed Owen.'

'I don't believe you.' Anna shouted, her words thick with grief. 'Todd wouldn't have done something like that. You're making it up.'

John shook his head. 'I'm afraid I'm not.' He turned back to Ellie. 'After that, it was damage limitation, and he had to be disposed of. I stabbed Todd and shoved him in the sea.'

Dave stepped forward. 'John Field, I am arresting you on suspicion of the murder of Todd Reynolds. You do not have to say anything, but it may harm your defence if you do not mention ...'

Chapter 42
THURSDAY

I t was November 5th, two days after the arrest of John and Gail Field, and George Oaks.

Ellie had left the electrician fitting a new consumer board at the windmill. She and Dave were on the village green with Rebus, who was pulling at his lead and squealing, tail wiggling.

'He's seen Sally,' said Ellie.

'Are you looking for Zoe?' Sally gave Ellie a huge hug and pointed at the ground, where two holes had been created in the bottom of the bonfire construction. 'She and Finn insist on searching for hedgehogs, toads and frogs.'

Ellie crouched down, laying a hand on the grass to steady herself and holding onto Rebus. 'Are there any in there?'

The early afternoon light was dropping, along with the temperature. Fortunately, the forecast was for a dry evening.

Zoe and Finn were on their hands and knees in the middle of the bonfire, gently trying to part the timber so as to be able to rescue any wildlife that was lurking within.

'One toad so far,' said Zoe, 'but I have a feeling there might be a hedgehog too. Finn and I saw one last night. We've got to search now, before it's dark, otherwise we won't see them. All we'll have time for later is to shine the torch quickly along the ground before the bonfire is lit.'

'I'm sure they'll appreciate it,' said Ellie.

'You have got hold of Reeby, haven't you?' asked Zoe.

'We have,' Ellie replied.

'We? Is dad here too?'

'Yup.'

'Is he coming to the fireworks?'

'I am,' said Dave. 'With your mother, your grandmother and your great-grandmother.'

'Yay.' Zoe poked her head out of the wood. 'Mary's coming too. And Sarge? And Reverend Jackson?'

Ellie couldn't help laughing. 'Yes. It *is* the village fireworks, Zoe, lovey. Everyone's going to be there. Including Gladys Blackman and her family.'

Zoe and Finn had been out all morning and Ellie hadn't had the chance to update them.

'The gnome is back on her husband's grave,' Ellie told Zoe. 'The doorbell footage identified Todd as the culprit.'

'Given Todd's dead, we can't verify this,' said Dave, 'but we suspect, from his choice of victims, and from what his mum told us, he was targeting people who'd upset him. Gladys because of the hind meat. Anna because she finished with him and Owen because he was the cause. John and Gail because he'll have known they were never going to let him control them for much longer. And I suspect the gnome outside the windmill was for me because he knows I've got CCTV at my place.'

As Ellie's comment about 'everyone being there' lingered on her lips, she felt a jab in the guts because *everyone* wasn't going to be there. There would be no Owen, no Todd, no John, no Gail and no George. And she wasn't sure whether Anna would be up to joining them, either.

'Reverend Jackson said how helpful you've been with his CCTV,' Dave told Zoe.

'Oh gosh. Sorry about the USB of the graveyard. Am I in trouble?'

'Technically, you shouldn't have done it, but he gave his permission, and your gran pressed the buttons. And – the main thing is, you didn't delete or alter the recording.'

'Phew. Sorry, Dad.'

'There's no point me saying don't do it again, because I know it falls on deaf ears as much with you as with your mum. And you helped Mrs Blackman to get the gnome back for her husband's grave.'

———ele———

Just under three hours later, the Blixes were setting off for the village fireworks and bonfire.

'Got everything?' Ellie asked Zoe.

'Yeah, Mum.'

'We'll come and collect you before the fireworks,' Ellie shouted at Mary and Sarge, who were staying in the windmill to conserve their energy and look after Rebus. She pulled the door shut.

'We'll probably come back and find they've dug a pond or started building a rockery,' said Zoe, grinning.

'Don't. Anything's possible with those two.'

Rebus would be fine in his bed in the office, with the curtains drawn and a lamp on, when they collected Mary and Sarge. It wasn't the fireworks he didn't like; more large crowds of moving people where he could get stepped on.

Dave zapped the locks on his Audi and joined them. 'So, we're getting torches from the butchers this year, is that right?' He wrapped his scarf around his neck and tied it into a loose knot. 'That's kind of Nick.' He produced a few boxes of sparklers from inside his jacket. 'Anyone else get any?'

'We did,' Zoe exclaimed. 'Apparently Todd has been selling a load of dodgy ones to the kids. They've all had to be recalled as they've led to burns.'

'That toerag has been selling illegal fireworks for the last three months as well,' Dave added. 'Managed to get a few lots into a couple of local garages, some into a youth centre and a football club.'

Ellie's thoughts ran to Anna, who was at home with her sister, getting ready for Owen's funeral. No one fully understood what had attracted her to Todd, but they'd obviously had a strong connection and it wasn't fair for people to reduce it to Todd simply being the opposite of Owen. There had to be more to it than that. Ellie knew Anna would be going over and over her choices and decisions, and she was aware of wanting to offer her friend kindness, rather than judgement.

Usually, Nick Matthews donated a pig to the village and Owen and his sous-chef roasted it on a spit outside the Windmill Inn during the afternoon, carrying it over to the green just before the bonfire was lit.

This year, though, it was going to be different. Alan from the village bistro had set up his outdoor pizza oven on the green, and Dave, Bob and Nick were going to be cooking burgers, chicken, sausages and jacket potatoes on Nick's fancy BBQ stove.

Every year, as far back as Ellie could remember, the village folk always collected their torches from outside the Windmill Inn. Tom and Maggie had always organised small ones for the children, larger ones for the adults. This year, though, everything had changed. The pub had only skeletal staff and was offering the bare minimum of services. Drinks only, no food.

Ellie returned to Dave's question. 'Yep, torches from Nick's shop, and the procession leaves the high street at 6pm, into Pennypot Lane, two laps of the village green followed by the lighting of the bonfire by the torchbearers.'

'Off we go then,' said Sylvia, pulling her beret down over her hair.

The Blixes strode along Pennypot Lane. Zoe had an arm linked through Finn's on one side and Sylvia's on the other.

An arm slipped through Ellie's. It was Dave's. For a moment, the gesture threw her.

Zoe turned round and caught her eye, grinning.

It felt nice to be close to Dave, to feel the warmth and movement of his body; to feel alive again.

Along the lane, a thin light fell from the occasional street lamps, just enough for them to be able to see where they were placing their feet, but not so much that the pumpkin lanterns left over from Halloween couldn't be seen, glowing a yellowy-orange in the semi-darkness.

They walked past a row of houses, all rendered and painted in a different colour. The pink one, where one of Ellie's cleaners lived with her family, had a huge spider's web across the inside of the window with a skeleton hanging from the curtain pole.

As they approached the residential home, staff in the day room were pushing furniture to one side so that residents would be able to watch the fireworks from inside.

'I'm going up to Birmingham next week,' said Dave casually.

Ellie felt as though a cold hand had reached inside her. 'Oh. OK. That just to have a look around, or...?'

'Sort of. It's to meet the boss who's offered me the position and to discuss what's needed for the new project.' He looked at her, his eyes shining.

Ellie felt the hand squeeze her guts. She wanted to be pleased for him. Wanted him to be happy.

'Sounds great.'

Say more. Keep him talking.

'For a while I thought about moving away too,' she said.

'What changed your mind? I'm finding it hard to decide what I want to do.'

'Zoe. Simon. Sylvia. The windmill...' She wanted to say *'you'*. Because he *had* been a reason why she hadn't wanted to leave; but he'd also been the reason she'd wanted to go.

Was this what Dave was hinting at? For her to tell him whether to stay or go? Or was he just updating her and sharing information, as she'd requested?

'Why don't you come with me?' he said gently.

She almost stopped walking but forced herself to continue. 'Are you being serious?'

'Yes. If you want to – why not? It's not far and it could be a new start for both of us, Ells, a way of moving on.' He patted her hand reassuringly. 'Anyway, no rush. I'm just putting it out there as an option. I haven't decided myself yet what I want to do so there's no pressure. If you fancy it, give me a shout. If you don't; no worries.'

Thoughts shot like arrows inside Ellie's mind. 'What about the kids? The windmill? Sylvia and Mary? Blix Blitz?'

Dave gave an understanding smile. 'That's the tricky bit, isn't it? What to do about all those people and situations?'

He gave a gentle chuckle. 'But the kids aren't kids anymore. They have their own lives and ...' He stopped. 'I don't want to try and persuade you, Ells. I've been doing that for a year. I'll leave it with you. Totally your call.'

After the torchlight procession, Zoe and Finn dashed off to do a last-minute wildlife check underneath the bonfire, and Dave went to join Nick and Bob on the barbecue.

Ellie and Sylvia collected Mary and Sarge from the windmill and brought them over to the green for the bonfire, food and fireworks.

The bonfire was lit and, for what seemed like ages afterwards, the locals stood around watching the effigy of Guy Fawkes burn, warming their hands and staring into the flames.

Zoe and Finn had joined them now.

'Fancy a burger?' Sylvia asked them all.

'Not particularly,' Ellie said, 'but I could eat some chicken. Zo?'

Zoe shook her head. 'I've ... um ... got some news.'

Ellie and Sylvia exchanged panicked glances.

'Your faces. No, I'm not pregnant and no, we aren't getting married. So, now it'll be a disappointment. I'm vegetarian. Ta da.'

A moving object shot into the sky and burst over their heads like a liquid umbrella of colour. Then another and four more: white, green, blue and red.

'That's brilliant, Zoe, love,' Ellie shouted over the bangs from the fireworks. 'If it's what you want, that's all that matters to your dad and me.'

'And Birmingham?' Zoe asked.

However hard Ellie found it sometimes, she respected that her daughter had things she cared passionately about; that she asked the hard questions that many others stayed silent on. Because it challenged Ellie to dig deep; to face her fears and to answer honestly.

'Birmingham isn't where I'm heading,' Ellie told her. 'As for your dad ...' She plonked a kiss on Zoe's forehead, 'I don't know because *he* doesn't. We'll just have to forge ahead with our own lives, and wait and see what he decides for his.'

The End.

If you enjoyed Ellie, Sylvia and Zoe's adventures in this book, do follow them in the next one, **Murder in the Hare Meadow**, which is available on Amazon here. The blurb is this:

A secret that won't stay buried. An escape artist rabbit. Three women sleuths.

It's spring in Lower Wootton and Ellie Blix has reluctantly started house-sitting for her cleaning clients. After a flurry of bookings, she's in charge of kittens and hamsters at the local pet shop.

When her daughter finds a dead body in the pond at the hare meadow, their tight-knit community is thrown into turmoil. The victim is identified as a local man who's just been released from prison. With a long list of people who might wish him harm, Ellie is relieved to leave the investigation to the police.

But evidence quickly casts suspicion on her detective inspector ex-husband, Dave, and Ellie and her sleuthing partners must find answers fast.

Then, a second death reveals a terrible truth from the past, one so personal it shakes Ellie to the core. To solve the murder, and return the village to safety, she must wrestle with her conscience and decide – did she ever really know Dave at all?

You can pre-order **Murder in the Hare Meadow** here.

A note from the author

Dear reader,

Thank you so much for reading this book. It has been a pleasure to write but, without you, it would simply be words in a document on my hard drive.

It is immensely gratifying that so many of you have taken the characters and stories from *The Wootton Windmill Mysteries* into your homes and hearts. Many of you have taken the time to email and tell me what the stories have meant to you. I read and reply to each one.

Getting news first

The best way to keep in touch is to join my newsletter. This is where I share news first, including exclusive offers, early reads, 'behind the scenes' & giveaways. You can join here.

Supporting the series

You can do this in three ways:

a) If you've enjoyed this story, please tell your friends, family, book clubs, and online groups about the series. It's easy to underestimate what this can do, but word of mouth is one of the best forms of marketing.

b) Another way to help is by leaving a quick, written review on Amazon. Amazon prompts us to leave a rating when we finish a book on kindle, and the average rating is important. However, a few lines saying what you liked about the story helps other readers to know what the book is like.

c) By pre-ordering the next in the series, which you can do here.

***

Please note: I am a British writer and I write using British English. This story is set in an English village and the manuscript has been edited and proofread by British professionals. A few spellings, terms and words may, therefore, be different for some readers. I've tried to ensure, however, that the meaning is clear for everyone.

Also – lots of people ask me if Lower Wootton is a real place. It isn't. It is a fictional village which I've created by borrowing elements of many villages, mixing them up and fictionalising them. If you try to plot places, you will find

I've moved them, changed them and given them different names!

Finally, writing a novel is a team effort. I come up with the plot and characters, and write the words, and other people contribute at various stages. Without their input and magic, this story would not have made it into print.

I owe massive thanks to the following people for their help. In no particular order: Lynne Nazareth, Louise Voss, Scott Pack, Ken Dawson, Lucy Lawrie, Liz Barnsley. Anne Coates. Linda and Alan Standen for help with local information. Richard Stone. Giles and Christine Camplin for help with hot air balloon information – all errors and creative licence are mine! Thanks also to Liz and Keith Atkinson who own Ripple Windmill, the inspiration for Ellie, Sylvia and Zoe's home in the series. To all my early and beta readers.

Sincere apologies to anyone I've forgotten.

About the Author

Izzie Harper is the pen name of British writer, teacher & story coach, Vicky Newham. Vicky lives on the south coast of England.

As Izzie Harper, she writes *The Wootton Windmill Mysteries*.

Vicky's first crime fiction series was published by HQ/Harper Collins. Her debut in this police procedural series, *Turn a Blind Eye*, was optioned for TV and was shortlisted for the CWA John Creasey Debut Dagger in 2019. She has MAs in Creative Writing and Effective Learning.

Vicky divides her time between writing and teaching. She is passionate about helping other writers to craft their stories, and to make informed decisions about their publishing paths.

To keep up to date with Vicky's releases, special offers and promotions, please join her newsletter here.

If you like pictures of dogs, the sea, the Kent countryside and behind-the-scenes of Vicky's writing, you can follow her on Twitter at @VickyNewham and on Instagram at @vickynewhamwriter.

If you have enjoyed this story, Vicky would be hugely grateful if you could leave a quick review on Amazon here and if you could tell your family and friends about it. Reviews and word-of-mouth recommendations are the best way to help authors.

And, please pre-order book 5, **Murder in the Hare Meadow**, here.

Printed in Great Britain
by Amazon